THE LEGEND OF RATTLER MINE

A MYSTERY SEARCHERS BOOK

BARRY FORBES

THE LEGEND OF RATTLER MINE

A MYSTERY SEARCHERS BOOK

Volume 9

BAKKEN
BOOKS

ISBN 978-1-955657-26-6
For Worldwide Distribution
Printed in the U.S.A.

Published by Bakken Books
2022

PRAISE FOR BARRY FORBES AND THE MYSTERY SEARCHERS FAMILY BOOK SERIES

AMAZING BOOK! My daughter is in 6th grade and she is homeschooled, she really enjoyed reading this book. Highly recommend to middle schoolers. *Rubi Pizarro on Amazon*

I have three boys 11-15 and finding a book they all like is sometimes a challenge This series is great! My 15-year-old said, "I actually like it better than Hardy Boys because it tells me currents laws about technology that I didn't know." My reluctant 13-year-old picked it up without any prodding and that's not an easy feat. *Shantelshomeschool on Instagram*

I stumbled across the author and his series on Instagram and had to order the first book! Fun characters, good storyline too, easy reading. Best for ages 11 and up. *AZmommy2011 on Amazon*

Virtues of kindness, leadership, compassion, responsibility, loyalty, courage, diligence, perseverance, loyalty and service are characterized throughout the book. *Lynn G. on Amazon*

Barry, he LOVED it! My son is almost 14 and enjoys reading but most books are historical fiction or non-fiction. He carried your book everywhere, reading in any spare moments. He can't wait for book 2 – I'm ordering today and book 3 for his birthday. *Ourlifeathome on Instagram*

Perfect series for our 7th grader! I'm thrilled to have come across this perfect series for my 13-year old son this summer. We purchased the entire set! They are easy, but captivating reads and he is enjoying them very much. *Amylcarney on Amazon*

Great "clean" page turner! My son was hooked after the first three chapters and kept asking me to read more... Fast forward three hours and we were done! When you read a book in one sitting, you know it is a good one. *Homework and Horseplay on Amazon*

"Great book for kids and no worry for parents! I bought and read this book with my grandson in mind. What a great book! The plot was well done using the sleuths' knowledge of modern technology to solve this mystery." *Regina Krause on Amazon*

"Take a break, wander away from the real world into the adventurous life of spunky kids out to save the world in the hidden hills of the Southwest." *Ron Boat on Amazon*

"Books so engaging my teenager woke up early and stayed up late to finish the story. After the first book, he asked: Are there more in this series? We HAVE to get them! He even chipped in some cash to buy more books." *Sabrinakaadventures on Instagram*

DISCLAIMER

Prescott, the former capital of the Arizona Territory, is considered by many to be the state's crown jewel. Aside from this Central Arizona locale, the Mystery Searchers Book series is a work of fiction. Names, characters, businesses, places, events, and incidents are either the products of the author's imagination or used in a fictitious manner. Any resemblance to actual persons, living or dead, or actual events is purely coincidental.

Read more at www.MysterySearchers.com

For Linda,
whose steadfast love and encouragement
made this series possible

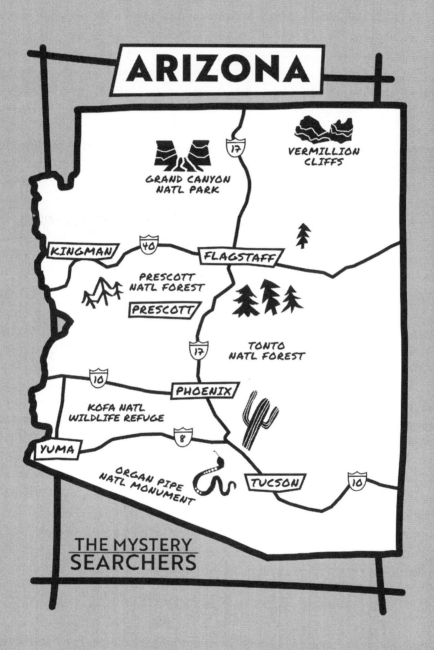

ARIZONA

GRAND CANYON NATL PARK

VERMILLION CLIFFS

KINGMAN 40 FLAGSTAFF

PRESCOTT NATL FOREST

PRESCOTT

17

TONTO NATL FOREST

10

PHOENIX

KOFA NATL WILDLIFE REFUGE

8

YUMA

ORGAN PIPE NATL MONUMENT

TUCSON 10

THE MYSTERY SEARCHERS

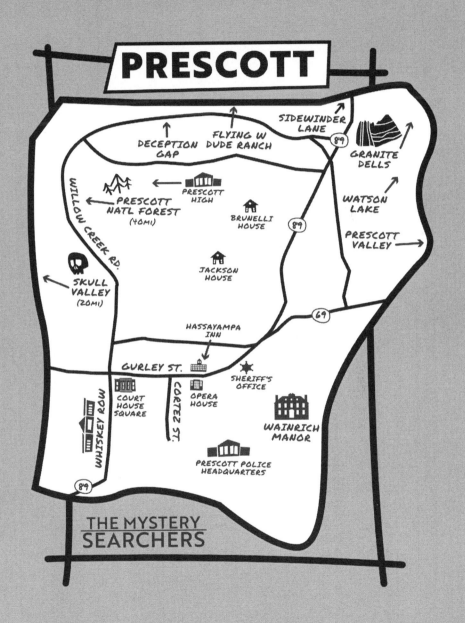

PRESCOTT

SIDEWINDER LANE

DECEPTION GAP

FLYING W DUDE RANCH

GRANITE DELLS

WILLOW CREEK RD.

PRESCOTT NATL FOREST (40MI)

PRESCOTT HIGH

BRUNELLI HOUSE

WATSON LAKE

PRESCOTT VALLEY

JACKSON HOUSE

SKULL VALLEY (20MI)

HASSAYAMPA INN

GURLEY ST.

CORTEZ ST.

SHERIFF'S OFFICE

COURT HOUSE SQUARE

WHISKEY ROW

OPERA HOUSE

WAINRICH MANOR

PRESCOTT POLICE HEADQUARTERS

THE MYSTERY SEARCHERS

89 · 89 · 69

1

VULTURES!

The mystery searchers raced their horses to the northern border of the Flying W Dude Ranch. They pulled up, side by side, their mounts panting, on a bluff overlooking undulating meadowlands broken by a series of canyons and ravines. The picture-perfect scenes before them were stunning.

"*Wow,*" Suzanne exclaimed. "Check. It. Out."

Meadow grass rustled in the breeze like silken waves. In the distance, mountains reached high into a brilliant sky as huge, puffy white clouds sailed across an ocean of Arizona blue. To the west, ponderosa pines arose, countless green sentinels that filled their eyes as far as they could see. At the bottom of the sharp drop-off below the bluff, cottonwoods dotted both sides of a running creek, too distant for them to hear the bubbling water.

They breathed deeply, enjoying the cool, fresh air that wafted down from the northern heights, carried by a gusting wind. No one said a word as they passed two canteens back and forth. Overhead, birds wheeled and screeched in the early afternoon. Their horses whinnied and stamped their hooves, eager to move on.

That's when Pete Brunelli startled everyone, pointing into the sky, and shouting, "Vultures!" Half a mile away, three raptors soared in wobbly circles above the rolling meadows, their wings tilted high enough to resemble a letter V.

"E-e-e-ew," Kathy exclaimed, pulling a face. "You're right. Nature's garbagemen! They're circling in for a landing. Has to be roadkill down there . . . somewhere. Yuck."

Born and raised in Central Arizona, the foursome knew all about the unsightly birds. Although their vast wingspan allowed them to fly and glide with a mere twitch of a wing, they weren't quite as graceful in defending themselves. The raptors' only defense against predators was to vomit all over them. And considering that they only eat dead meat, well . . .

"Roadkill? No way," Pete replied, never reluctant to argue with his sister. "There isn't a road for miles. Who's got the binoculars?"

The twins, Tom and Suzanne Jackson, glanced at each other. "I do," Suzanne said. She reached into her saddlebags and retrieved a set. Within seconds, she focused on the three vultures as they continued to hover, riding thermals in wide circles. Two species of the birds make Arizona their summer home, and they're quite similar.

"What are they, Suzie?" Tom asked. He was the thoughtful, quiet one of the four.

"Turkey vultures." Through the binoculars, the species was easily identifiable by its bald, red head and pinkish bill, and a black-and-grey wingspan that could often exceed five feet. Suzanne knew that they migrated north from Mexico every spring and returned in the fall—and that they can smell carrion from an incredible eight miles away. She handed the binoculars to Pete.

2

Kathy held one hand out toward her brother. "Gimme." He ignored her for the longest time, earning a withering look.

Then, without warning, Pete—always the impulsive one—nudged the flanks of his fast, chestnut-colored gelding and galloped off, shouting, "Let's go see what they're after!"

The mystery searchers had won a week's stay at the Flying W, located a few miles northwest of Prescott. Heidi Hoover—a good friend and the star reporter of *The Daily Pilot*, Prescott's hometown newspaper—had recommended the foursome for the prize. Their work on solving a recent kidnapping-and-ransom case had made national headlines. With a little help from Heidi, the four had helped track down the crime's elusive mastermind.

The *Pilot* had awarded its Citizen of the Year Award to the four friends. It was the first time the paper had ever honored a group rather than an individual with the much-coveted prize. The mystery searchers couldn't believe their luck.

"I *love* horses," Suzanne had said when Heidi called to share the good news. "I can't wait!"

A grin crossed Tom's face. "The ranch's wranglers are known for working their guests half to death."

"I can handle it." She could too. Often when friends thought of the outgoing girl, one word came to mind: *confident*. She knew where she was going in life, and how to get there.

Prescott, a small Central Arizona city nestled in a mile-high basin among pine-dotted mountains, boasts hundreds of miles of riding trails. It's also home to "the world's oldest rodeo"—cowboy country, for sure.

As the foursome had soon discovered, a week at the Flying W Dude Ranch was no picnic. Rather, it was an intensive course on how to feed, water, groom, saddle and bridle, mount, ride, walk, trot, canter, and dismount a horse. *Whew!*

Now Friday had arrived, along with their final ride. Each of them had admitted to loving every minute of the experience. Or most of it, anyway. Cleaning up after the horses in the barn—mucking out their stalls—wasn't as much fun as riding them and handing out treats.

"It hasn't all been peaches and cream," Kathy reminded her brother—her favorite target for good-natured teasing—with a giggle. "Remember when you fell off Trigger?"

Pete chortled. "Time out! Trigger and I are old friends now."

In a way, that was true. The Flying W wranglers had paired each of them with their own mount for the duration. Horse and rider had soon grown to know each other, and what to expect. Best of all, the dude ranch reserved mornings for chores and riding lessons. Afternoons were free for riding the range from one o'clock on. *Delicious.*

Pete led, yipping and yahooing down the left side of the bluff and onto the meadowlands. Trigger coursed across familiar territory as he galloped over the grasslands without a second's hesitation, heading toward endless canyons and ravines that gathered in front. As they grew closer to the first ravine, the horse slowed.

"Hold up, Pete!" his sister yelled from behind. Kathy's dark-bay quarter horse was a gentle beast that liked to ramble rather than run. All Kathy had to say was "Whoa," and he slowed to a halt.

The twins, riding a pair of young mares—Tom's a palomino he had nicknamed Goldie, and his sister's a strawberry roan—caught up with their best friends. "Check out the birds," Suzanne said. "They're still circling. What are they waiting for?"

"Dinner," Kathy quipped. "And whatever's on the menu isn't far away."

Tom cut to the right, heading northeast, searching for a safe path around a steep, narrow gorge that appeared risky. The foursome traveled together in silence as the sure-footed horses trotted along. A few hundred yards farther on, the gorge merged into a navigable, rock-filled chasm with gently sloping sides that soon returned them to the meadowlands.

"Hooray!" Pete yelled, leaving the others in a cloud of dust.

Minutes later, the horses began slowing once more as another ravine lay ahead. The raptors were almost directly overhead now, still circling, gradually working their way lower. The four riders dismounted and walked closer to the edge.

Kathy stopped dead in her tracks as she peered down into the abyss. One hand flew to her mouth. "Oh, my Lord. There's a body down there—a human body!"

Suzanne blanched. "There surely is."

Pete and Tom gazed down, jolted into silence.

The steep ravine wall slanted downward at a sharp angle. Right at the bottom, maybe fifteen yards down, lay a heavy-set, bareheaded man with a bushy red beard, face up, one arm folded over his chest, the other resting at his side. He wore jeans and a long-sleeved shirt.

"Looks like he's sleeping," Kathy said.

Pete shook his head. "Naw, I think he's a goner."

"I doubt it," Tom said. He grabbed a rope attached to his saddle and looped the strap of a canteen around his neck.

"Why not?" Pete asked.

"The vultures, remember? They only eat carrion. And they haven't landed. Yet."

"Oh, got it," Pete replied. "I'm going down with you."

"No way," Suzanne said. "You're riding the fastest horse. No matter whether the guy's dead or alive, we'll need help. Tom and I'll handle it."

"What the heck," Pete objected. "That's what cellphones are for. It's called nine-one-one."

"Good luck with that, buddy," Kathy retorted, whipping her phone out of her pocket to check for a signal. "Cellphone service out here in the meadowlands is pretty patchy, and right here . . . zip."

"Well, that's awkward," Pete said, disappointment heavy in his voice. That hadn't crossed his mind. *"Duh."*

Tom tied one end of the rope to a dead tree on the edge of the ravine. "It'll get us down ten feet at the most, but it's a good start."

Broken rocks of every shape and size lined the ravine's walls, protruding from the packed earth. The twins used them for footholds as they climbed down, testing each one before putting weight on it. A few smaller rocks pushed loose and thundered downhill, one almost rolling over the helpless man.

"Geez," Tom muttered to himself. "That was close."

Three minutes later, they fell to their knees before the red-bearded man. He appeared to be in his fifties, unconscious, and badly hurt.

But alive.

"He's still breathing," Suzanne murmured, watching his chest rise and fall. "But pale as a ghost." His forehead felt cool to the touch.

The twins noticed bloody abrasions on the man's head, neck, arms, and hands. A great deal of blood had pooled below his upper back. Worse, it had begun coagulating along one side.

"He must have rolled down into the ravine," Tom said. "And recently too."

Suzanne agreed. "Fallen . . . or been pushed. His clothes are damp. How come?"

"Might be sweat from being out in the sun. How on earth would he get all the way out here? We're so far from —anywhere."

"Maybe he came on horseback, like us, but his horse ran off," Suzanne said.

Tom unscrewed the canteen lid and poured a tiny amount of water over the man's lips. He shuddered as his eyes flickered open. A few seconds passed before he focused on Suzanne's face. He struggled to speak, licking his lips. The twins leaned closer.

"I—I, uh . . . It's there . . . I found it . . ." His eyes flickered once more, then closed.

For one horrifying moment, Suzanne thought he had died. But he continued to breathe in shallow gasps.

Tom lifted the man's arms one at a time, gently palpating his chest and the sides of his ribcage with the fingertips of one hand. *Nothing.* He slid his hands under both shoulders and felt around.

Suzanne swiveled her head and glanced up at the Brunellis, peering down from the top of the ridge. She cupped her mouth, shouting, *"He's alive!* And hurt badly! We need a medical helicopter—but it won't be able to land in the ravine!"

"Tell 'em they'll have to lower a stretcher down there," Kathy said to her brother.

"Okay, I'm on it!" Pete yelled back. He bounded into his saddle.

"And while you're at it, call Sheriff McClennan!" Tom called out. *"Somebody shot this guy!"*

2

RESCUE

Organized pandemonium soon broke out on the edge of a nameless ravine north of the Flying W.

Pete had returned with Rob Rhinehart, the owner of the dude ranch, and two of his wranglers, Gary Brown and Frank Hanson, tall, lanky guys with easy dispositions. The mystery searchers had worked closely with them all week long. Cowboying was a way of life, and the men reveled in it. Both were the very image of the classic cowboy, from their well-worn cowboy boots to their wide-brimmed Stetsons.

Rob was a smaller, wiry mirror of his two ranch hands—rugged and square-jawed, with jeans, boots, and a cowboy hat—right down to his western drawl and tanned face. Born on the ranch, Rob told anyone who would listen that he'd die there too.

The men had trailed Pete, galloping across the grasslands and circling the ravines. They arrived just ahead of the helicopter, hearing it long before a tiny dot appeared in the sky. Rob and his two ranch hands led all the horses to a nearby oasis to prevent the chopper's whirling blades from spooking them.

Yavapai County's Search and Rescue helicopter was soon sweeping low overhead, its pilot surveying the terrain for a safe landing spot.

"That noise is incredible!" Kathy bellowed. "Plus, it's really messing with my hair!"

Pete's eyes flicked over to his sister. "I hope you're kidding!" he said with a certain look.

The pilot performed a tight three-sixty before setting the chopper down fifteen yards from the edge of the ravine, churning up a stinging whirlwind of fine brown dust. Even before the screaming rotors slowed to a stop, the copter's doors sprang open as uniformed personnel jumped out and raced over.

Without a word, three paramedics and a nurse tied ropes to the same dead tree Tom had used. They attached a folded, lightweight gurney to one rope and lowered it carefully to the bottom of the ravine. Then they rappelled down the side —all within just seconds. The mystery searchers were impressed.

Two other passengers dropped to the ground. Sheriff Steve McClennan, a large, beefy man in a khaki uniform, joined Pete and Kathy on the edge of the chasm. Detective Derek Robinson—"Derek" to the mystery searchers—ran past them and rappelled down behind the rescue team.

The foursome had known the sheriff since childhood. As they entered high school, they had helped the Sheriff's Office to solve a couple of mysteries. And when Derek joined the force, they had teamed up with him on the Sidewinder Lane case, which had led them to discover a long-forgotten bank heist. A quiet, unassuming investigator of medium height,

Derek had distinctive red hair that stood out like a beacon. Freckles covered every inch of his visible skin.

"Whadda we got?" the sheriff growled.

"An unconscious man," Kathy replied. "We spotted turkey vultures circling and rode over to see what they were after."

"That's how we found him," Pete added. "Tom says he's got a bullet hole in him."

Rob and the two wranglers made their way back, having left the horses tethered by a nearby watering hole. Turned out that Rob and Sheriff McClennan were old friends from high school.

Rob extended his hand. "Hey, Steve, how ya doing?"

"Fine, good to see you, Rob. Any idea who this guy is?"

"Never seen him before. Pete told us someone used him for target practice."

"I heard."

"It's weird that he's even out here," Mr. Rhinehart added. "Few people ever ride this far north. We're smack in the middle of nowhere."

Pete and Kathy introduced the two wranglers to the sheriff. Meanwhile, down below, the paramedics had stemmed the unknown man's bleeding and bandaged his multiple abrasions. They'd had to cut off his shirt to lift him enough to wrap a big white bandage around his torso. Soon, they slid his unconscious body onto the gurney.

"Okay, start bringing him up!" the nurse yelled from below. "Slow and easy—we'll keep him level!"

Pete and Kathy walked over to the dead tree to help. Together, they released the ropes as everyone grabbed a section and stepped back.

"*Slower!*" the nurse yelled.

Two minutes passed before the gurney slid over the ridgeline. The rescue team clamored to the top, with

Suzanne, Tom, and Derek close behind. The rescuers stopped to gather their breath before rushing their patient over to the helicopter. With an odd whining sound, the rotors returned to life and began whirling ever faster. Soon enough, the copter lifted into the air—creating earsplitting noise and generating another dust storm—before it executed a one-eighty and turned toward Prescott.

In the dead silence that followed, the mystery searchers gathered around Derek and Sheriff McClennan.

"How's he look?" the sheriff asked.

"Not good," Derek replied. "He's unconscious and they couldn't get any response. The nurse said it's fifty-fifty that he'll make it."

"Someone wanted him dead," the sheriff grunted.

"That's a fact. He took two shots. One went in his back high up and on the right, between the shoulder blades. The bullet went right through him, he's lucky it didn't hit a lung. A second one grazed his ribcage on the right side. The paramedics found this"—he held up a small plastic evidence bag containing a single bullet—"in the earth underneath him. They said he's lost a massive amount of blood."

The sheriff stared hard at Derek. "Someone shot him in the *back?*"

"Yes, sir."

"Must've crept up and taken him by surprise—" said Tom.

"Unless he was running from the person who shot him," said Kathy.

"We think that person might've pushed him over the edge too," Suzanne added. "He had abrasions on his head, neck, arms and hands."

"Maybe he was near the edge," Pete surmised. "and the force of the first bullet made him stagger and fall over."

"That must've hurt," the sheriff grunted, glancing downward. "It's a long way to the bottom."

"We found his wallet," Tom said. "His name is Herbert W. Wakefield, and he's fifty-six years old."

"He has a rural address outside Wickenburg," the detective said. He turned the wallet around to display its contents. Inside was a twenty-dollar bill, but no credit cards. An Arizona driver's license displayed a grandfatherly image of a smiling man with a bushy red beard. "Wickenburg's just an hour south of Prescott. I'll drive out there later today and check for family. I'll need a car."

"Yeah, I've got two of them coming to the ranch," the sheriff said. "I have to return to headquarters." He stopped for a second in thought. "Wakefield didn't have a cellphone?"

"Not on him," Derek replied. "I'll check to see if there's a cell in his name."

Rob Rhinehart and his two ranch hands had gathered around, listening to the conversation. Frank Hanson, spoke up. "You can use our horses, Sheriff. When you get to the Flying W, ask whoever's in the stable to bring 'em back here for us."

"Okay, thanks Frank. Appreciate it."

Meanwhile, Tom searched the ground along the ridgeline. He bent over before calling out, "There's a shell casing over here!"

The other mystery searchers raced over, followed by Derek and the sheriff.

"Sure enough," Derek said. He reached down and picked up the piece of evidence with a handkerchief. "It's a .30/06 Winchester. Let's see if we can find another one nearby." The six of them paced back and forth in parallel lines, slowly retreating away from the edge of the ravine. Soon, the sheriff enlisted the help of Rob and the two wranglers. Together, the group scanned every square inch of the ridgeline and the land behind it. They covered an area a good fifty yards on each side.

Nothing.

"Whoever fired the shots must've taken the other shell," the sheriff said.

"Or else," said Tom, "they shot Mr. Wakefield somewhere else, then brought his body over here and dumped him down into the ravine."

"Two shots were fired—one that grazed him, one that almost killed him," Suzanne said. "Which came first? The second shot could have been fired down into the ravine, if Mr. Wakefield landed face down—"

Just then, Gary Brown yelled, "Sheriff, check this out!"

"What is it?"

"Two horses rode up here." He pointed down to parallel tracks of hoofprints in the dust. "The trailing horse has a distinctive horseshoe, with one bent nailhead sticking out of the bottom surface."

Derek unfolded a pocket-size miniature ruler. He set it beside the imprint before grabbing a couple of pics with his cellphone. "Any possibility it belongs to one of your horses?"

"Not a chance," Frank replied. "We're awful careful about things like that."

Sheriff McClennan brightened. His family had a long history with horses. "We just caught a break, Derek. A farrier nails on a horseshoe so that each nailhead is countersunk into a slot in the bottom surface of the shoe. Whoever nailed this shoe in place messed up. One nail is protruding a bit, and the horse's own weight has bent the nailhead so it digs down into the ground with every step. It's like a fingerprint—if we locate that horse, we've found our shooter."

"That's a fact," Rob agreed. "You don't see a bent nail that's sticking out too often."

"So what happened to Mr. Wakefield's horse?" Tom asked.

"Me and Frank will ride the range," Gary offered. "If it's out here, we'll find it."

"If it is Mr. Wakefield's horse," Suzanne figured out loud, "he must've brought it from Wickenburg. That means his vehicle and horse trailer can't be far away."

"Good point," the sheriff said. "I'll have deputies scout up and down the old mining trails. It'll take time—there's a lot of 'em. The crime scene crew is on the way. They'll go over this area with a fine-tooth comb."

"One thing," Derek said. "Wakefield spoke a few words to the twins."

McClennan shifted his eyes over to them. "Oh, yeah? He was conscious?"

"Not until we poured water on his lips," Tom explained. "His eyes opened, and he said something. We weren't sure what he meant."

"What'd he say?"

"He said, 'It's there,'" Suzanne replied.

"And then he said, 'I found it,'" Tom added.

A shocked expression crossed Rob's face. "He said he *found* it?"

"Yes, sir," Suzanne replied.

Rob's head pivoted toward the sheriff. "Do you—does that mean what I think it means?"

"Well . . . I—sure, it's just a guess, and I can't believe it. That legend has been floating around my whole life."

"What is it, Sheriff?" Pete asked. *Interesting.*

"The legend of Rattler Mine." The sheriff squinted off into the distance. "Story goes that a prospector discovered a deposit that could have been the richest gold mine in Arizona history. Back in the 1880s, I think . . . a large pocket quite near the surface, next to a stream. A cave with a hidden entrance and a big load of nuggets. Crystalline gold, it's called, and Arizona's not known for it. It's the rarest kind of gold nugget. Real pretty. Not eroded, like placer gold nuggets. You'll find 'em in Nevada and California."

Rob nodded. "Yup. Colorado too. But the prospector who made the strike and started digging disappeared before he could securely stake the claim—taking the location to the grave. Some people figured a rattler got him . . . that's where the name came from."

Kathy shuddered. She hated snakes with a passion.

The twins exchanged knowing looks. "Oh, sure," Suzanne said. "We remember Dad telling us about that."

"Right around here," the sheriff said. He stretched an arm out toward the northern horizon. "This place is riddled with old gold and silver claims. Hey, you never know. Stranger things have happened."

Rob chuckled. "That gold deposit has proved elusive for a century and a half. It'd be a miracle if this guy found it."

"Someone shot him for a reason," Derek said. "And whatever that reason was, Mr. Wakefield might die from it."

THE CRIME SCENE CREW SOON ARRIVED BY POLICE HELICOPTER. The mystery searchers observed the technicians closely, as they did at every opportunity. A couple hours inched by as the techs surveyed the site, but their work quickly ground to a halt.

They had a man, barely alive, with a bullet lodged in his back. . . one .30/06 shell casing on the ridgeline . . . a spent bullet under the victim at the bottom of the ravine . . . and his wallet with a driver's license and a twenty-dollar bill.

But hoofprints from a horseshoe with a bent, extended nailhead—they were a big deal. And so were Herbert Wakefield's halting words that might—*might*—explain why he had been found lying abandoned in a ravine, his life ebbing away in the middle of nowhere—until the mystery searchers discovered him . . .

"How about coming to Wickenburg with me in the morning?" Derek asked the foursome—all mounted on their horses, ready to return to the ranch. "Mr. Wakefield has a rural address. If he lives on an acreage, I could use a little help walking the land to look for clues."

"Oh, you bet," Pete said, grinning like crazy.

3

_____

WICKENBURG

T he twins sat with their parents after a late dinner, discussing their amazing week at the Flying W. They related how the horseback training had turned out even better than they could have imagined.

"Best week ever," Suzanne proclaimed, "until . . ." The story about the circling vultures and the unfortunate Mr. Wakefield tumbled out.

"Talk about the unexpected," Tom said.

"I looked over the ridge," Suzanne said, "and there he was. Lying right at the bottom of that steep-sided ravine. Pete figured he was deader than a doornail."

Their mother, Sherri, shook her head. "What a terrible thing. The poor man."

Their father—Chief Edward Jackson of the Prescott City Police, known to almost one and all as "the Chief"—focused, naturally enough, on the crime. But Sherri—an at-home social worker for Yavapai County—drilled right down to the danger zone. To the twins, it always seemed her two favorite words were *dangerous* and *risky*. A third one she often bandied about was *caution*. But they loved their mother dearly.

"I hope you're not getting involved in this case," she exhorted them. "I don't like the idea of some creep running around with a rifle—with you on his tail. Let the sheriff handle this one."

"Oh, Mom—" Suzanne started.

"Oh, Mom, nothing!" Sherri cut in, pursing her lips.

"Detective Robinson invited us to walk the man's acreage in the morning," Tom mentioned, almost in passing. "With him, of course."

"Here we go again," Sherri protested, rolling her eyes.

"You told us about the legend of Rattler Mine years ago," Suzanne said, glancing toward her father as she attempted to change the subject.

The twins both had their heart set on law enforcement careers, something the Chief encouraged at every opportunity. "Uh-huh. As a kid growing up in Prescott, that legend was a big deal. One weekend, our Boy Scout group camped out there. We spent the better part of a Saturday hiking around, searching for the mine's entrance." He chuckled. "Had a great time. We found a good-size rattlesnake, but no gold."

"We wondered how Mr. Wakefield ended up in the ravine," Tom said.

"Well, as you have already deduced, he either fell or was pushed," the Chief said. "If Mr. Wakefield pulls through, he'll have an interesting story to tell. Did the sheriff find any clues?"

"Tom found one shell casing near the edge of the ravine," Suzanne recalled, "and the EMTs found a bullet underneath Mr. Wakefield's back. And his wallet identified him. But there *was* one really good clue. The horse trailing behind the victim had a distinctive horseshoe, with one bent nailhead sticking out of the bottom surface. The sheriff figures the hoofprint will serve like a fingerprint."

"Great!" the Chief said, a smile crossing his face. "I'll bet anything that'll turn out to be a big deal."

"No one mentions Rattler Mine much these days," Tom said. "The Brunellis had never heard of it."

"Not surprising," their father replied. He took another sip of his coffee. "It's a long time past. When I was a kid, it was already nothing more than a legend. Kind of like searching for a pirate's treasure chest. It might exist, but who ever found one?"

"And no one has ever found Rattler Mine either," Suzanne declared.

"That could hold true, especially if Mr. Wakefield doesn't make it," the Chief added.

"Do we know if he's still unconscious?" Tom asked.

"Well, it's Sheriff McClennan's case," the Chief said, shifting in his chair. "He'll let us know if there's any change. But Wakefield was unconscious an hour ago. The man is in pretty rough shape."

"So sad," Sherri said. "He's lying in a hospital with no friends to care about him."

Suzanne turned to her mother. "That's where we come in."

EARLY ON SATURDAY MORNING, BEFORE HEADING OFF FOR Wickenburg, the mystery searchers called Derek to ask his permission for Heidi Hoover to join in the search.

"No problem," the detective said. "She can ride out with me. I just received a call from Frank Hanson at the Flying W. They found Mr. Wakefield's horse wandering around the meadowlands and brought her back to their stables. One of our crime scene techs is heading out to check for evidence."

"Anything on his vehicle and horse trailer?" Pete asked.

"Not yet. Deputies are still searching. There's a passel of old mining roads on that land. It could take a while."

Fifteen minutes later, Heidi Hoover pulled up to the Jacksons' home and parked behind the Brunellis' Mustang. The star newspaper reporter had shared in many of their previous adventures. Over cups of steaming hot coffee, the foursome brought her up to date on their latest case.

"*Sheesh,*" Heidi lamented. "They helicoptered him to the hospital? I wish you'd had cell service out there. I would have come right out. I'm tight with the guy who flies the traffic helicopter."

"No such luck," Suzanne said. "Pete had to ride back to the ranch just to call for medical help."

"Is the man still breathing?"

"So far," Pete replied. The Brunellis' mother, Maria, an emergency-room registered nurse, worked the day shift at Prescott Regional Medical Center, the city's largest hospital. She had filled them in earlier. "He's in Intensive Care, and it's touch and go. He lost way too much blood."

Heidi wrote furiously in her notebook. "Tell me about the legend of Rattler Mine."

"Not a lot to tell," Kathy said. "I spent an hour Googling the darn thing and came up with one mention. Guess where I found it?"

"*The Daily Pilot,* of course," Heidi replied with a hint of pride. "Makes sense. Outside Prescott, the story wouldn't generate much interest."

"Unless it's true," Tom said.

"If it's true—and *if* Mr. Wakefield found this famous, forgotten, long-hidden mine—it'd be a national story." Heidi said. Then she laughed, her tight black curls bouncing around her head. "And I'd get a raise!"

"Well, you guessed it," Kathy said to the diminutive reporter, whose stature belied her enormous energy. "A story appeared in the *Pilot* back in 1982. It mentioned Rattler Mine as part of Prescott's gold and silver mining history. Whoever wrote the article passed it off as nothing more than a legend."

"Told 'ya," Pete murmured, clearly irritating his sister.

"You did not."

Heidi grinned. "Written by one of my predecessors. Anything else?"

"Just the bare bones," Tom related, "which we already knew from the Chief. A local prospector had discovered the gold and started digging out the mine but disappeared before he could register the claim."

"Nothing but speculation," Pete said.

Kathy kicked her brother under the kitchen table. "You're being negative. That doesn't square with what Mr. Wakefield said."

"Did the story mention what happened to the prospector?" Heidi asked.

"They never found the guy," Suzanne related. "He just vanished without a trace. Back then, someone figured a rattler had got him. That's where the name came from." She paused. "Supposedly, a handful of gold nuggets from Rattler Mine made their way to the marketplace. The story claimed they were quite valuable."

"Imagine if *we* rediscovered that mine," Pete said, rubbing his hands together gleefully. "How amazing would that be?"

"Maybe Mr. Wakefield thought he already had," Tom said.

Suzanne blanched. "And maybe so did whoever shot him."

.   .   .

NINETY MINUTES LATER, THE JACKSONS' WHITE CHEVY TURNED hard right onto a rough gravel road three miles east of Wickenburg. Suzanne was at the wheel as their vehicle jolted along, following behind Derek's unmarked police sedan. Heidi sat in his front seat, riding with the detective.

A swirling cloud of dust floated upward, enveloping the white car in a brown haze. Pete and Kathy bounced around in the backseat.

"Hey, take it easy," Pete complained.

"Sorry!"

They had made the trip in just over an hour, taking 89 south out of Prescott and dropping down a series of mountain switchbacks to the desert floor below. The two sedans passed through a trio of small towns—Peoples Valley, Yarnell, Congress—before driving through Wickenburg and heading west into desolate land.

"There's gotta be a fair number of rattlers out here," Kathy noted. She pressed her nose against the window and stared out into the barren land.

A smirk crossed Pete's face. His sister's fear of snakes was family lore. "Deal with it."

A small ramshackle house appeared off the south side of the gravel road. Behind it, to the right, sat a garage with an open door, the kind that retracts upward. And behind the garage stood a small stable, which looked big enough to house maybe three horses, tops. Saguaro sentinels dotted the desert-flat landscape.

Derek turned left onto a dirt road and stopped parallel to Mr. Wakefield's front door. Suzanne pulled the Chevy up beside him. Dust rose behind them, driven by a furnace-like eastward-blowing wind. The outside temperature on the car read 105 degrees. The six of them stepped into the scorching heat.

"Whew," Pete complained. "It's already freaking hot out here."

"Get used to it," Kathy said, biting her lip.

Derek's eyes took in the scene. "We're not the first ones here."

"What do you mean?" Tom asked.

"When I left yesterday evening, I closed the garage door."

Uh-oh, Suzanne thought.

4

THE ACREAGE

They had just reached the house when another vehicle came bumping along the road.

The group turned to see a black SUV that had seen better days turn onto Wakefield's acreage and pull up behind the Chevy. A small, slim woman with a tanned face who appeared to be in her sixties, dressed in jeans and a short-sleeve blouse, opened the driver's side door and climbed out —with a bit of effort. She hesitated a few seconds, staring hard at the strangers.

"Who are you and what do you want?" she called out.

Derek walked over, pulling out his badge and holding it toward her. "I'm Detective Derek Robinson with the Yavapai County Sheriff's Office. May I ask your name, ma'am?"

"I'm Cynthia Myers," she replied, stepping back a foot. She crossed her arms and frowned. Clearly, she didn't much appreciate police officers. One hand strayed up to her white hair which, though cut short, was getting blown around by the hot wind. "What's going on?"

"Are you a friend of Mr. Wakefield's?" Derek asked.

"I am. His next-door neighbor too. I live just a short way up the road. So what?"

"You're not related?"

"Herb has no living relatives. What's this all about? Is he okay?"

"Well, he's in the hospital in Prescott," Derek replied, never taking his eyes off her. "I'm afraid there's been an incident."

She sagged. "Oh, my goodness. A snake got him, didn't it? I warned him."

Minutes later, as they all sat at a shaded picnic table behind Mr. Wakefield's house, the six visitors brought Cynthia—as she insisted they call her—up to speed. After recovering from the shocking news that Herb—Mr. Wakefield—had suffered two gunshot wounds, Cynthia settled down and seemed to accept Derek. Suzanne judged her to be a resilient person with a big heart, despite her initial prickliness.

"Poor Herb. Life hasn't been easy on him. He rarely talked about his past, but the man lived out here for a quarter century, eking out a livelihood prospecting for gold. He always discovered enough to get by. But I swear if I didn't bring food out here, he'd never eat a decent meal. Say, where's his horse?"

"The wranglers at the Flying W found her wandering in the meadowlands," Derek explained. "They brought her back to their stables. They're happy to care for her for a while."

"Thank goodness," Cynthia said with a deep sigh. "Herb loves Sugarcane. She's his best friend."

"Sugarcane?" Suzanne asked. "That's her name?"

"Yup. She's ten years old and gentle as a lamb."

Tom wondered, "Did Mr. Wakefield have any enemies?"

"Herb? *Never.* He's the type that would give you the shirt

off his back. I've seen him bring complete strangers home. He'd pick 'em up off the highway, many of them broke, down on their luck. I told him he shouldn't do that, but that's Herb for you." She paused, lost in thought. "Hey, maybe one of them got him."

"Doubtful," Derek said. "Given the circumstances in which he was discovered, whoever shot Mr. Wakefield more than likely knew him."

Suzanne caught her eye. "Cynthia, when Tom and I gave him water, he opened his eyes for a few seconds. He said, 'I found it.' Does that make any sense to you?"

"Oh, sure," she replied, brightening a little. "It's the legend of Rattler Mine. Herb's obsessed with it, always has been. He mentioned it to me twenty-five years ago, right after we met. Last week, when I dropped off my homemade lasagna— that's his favorite—he felt sure he had found the mine. I've never seen him so excited."

"Did you believe him?" Heidi asked.

Cynthia tilted her head back in surprise. "Believe him? *Of course I did.* Herb's a straight shooter. Whether it was the real Rattler Mine, that's a different story, but Herb thought so. He even showed me some ore samples. Said it was the richest he had ever seen in a quarter century. Of course, I wouldn't know rich ore if it bit me on the nose, but they sure looked pretty. Big crystals of gold in them."

"Any idea where those samples are now?" Pete asked.

"In the house, I guess. Let's go see—Herb never locks his doors."

"I was here last night," Derek said. "He had them lined up on the kitchen table."

Heidi and the mystery searchers trooped in behind Derek, with Cynthia leading, taking her time. They squeezed into a tiny rectangular kitchen with a small table in the middle.

Derek stopped. "Well, that's interesting. Someone's been here and helped themselves to the ore samples."

"They sure have," Cynthia said. "What the heck is going on?"

"I'm pretty sure someone wants that gold mine to disappear," Tom said.

Pete nodded. "Again."

Derek turned toward Cynthia. "I arrived here last night around six o'clock. Did you hear me driving in?"

"Uh-huh. I figured it was Herb and paid no attention. But I spotted you leaving and realized it wasn't him. I called his cellphone, but there was no answer—it went straight into voicemail."

"You heard no one else?" Pete asked.

"Nope. But I'm fast asleep before ten." Her eyes circled the kitchen. "Whoever swiped the samples came later."

THE NEXT TWO HOURS DRAGGED BY AS THE HEAT CLIMBED EVER higher. The mystery searchers searched the garage and the stable. It turned out that Mr. Wakefield kept everything in its place. In the garage, his workbench sat empty, all his tools stored in drawers or dangling from a pegboard. Garden and landscape equipment hung from the ceiling or rested against the walls. Even the stable had been swept clean.

Despite sunhats, the foursome sweat profusely as they walked the acreage in parallel lines, north and south, then east and west. The man kept a clean five-acre parcel of land —no junk anywhere. Just rocks, cacti, and heat. The temperature on Tom's cellphone read 112 degrees.

"Snakes," Kathy muttered to herself. Flat desert terrain

made it easy to search ahead—no grass. There were, however, *hundreds* of rocks, which Kathy skirted at every opportunity. But no snakes. "That we can *see*," she insisted. "Doesn't mean they're not here."

Meanwhile, the others—Derek, Heidi, and Cynthia— searched the ramshackle cabin, looking for anything that might represent a clue. At one point, Heidi found a framed fifty-year-old picture of a young man riding a bucking bronco, tucked between two books on a small bookshelf in the tiny, neat bedroom. At the top of the image was the date and a caption: *World's Oldest Rodeo, Prescott, Arizona.* And at the bottom, *National Champion Herb Wakefield Wins Again!*

An astonished Cynthia said, "He never mentioned it. Not once. But he always loved horses."

Later, the mystery searchers returned to the cabin's front door—hot, sweating, and bedraggled. There wasn't really room for seven people inside the tiny home, so Heidi walked out with the photograph in hand. "Here's something interesting. This guy was a real cowboy."

Derek's cellphone buzzed. A brief conversation ensued before he stepped outside too.

"A deputy located Mr. Wakefield's truck and trailer. She didn't spot anything obviously unusual, but they'll move 'em to the impound lot and check them out, sweep for prints and fibers, all that. One thing, uh, I should mention. The crime lab reported blood on his saddle."

"Whoa, that's not good," Pete said grimly. "If his assailant shot him before dumping his body into the ravine, he must have been bleeding for a very long time."

Cynthia fainted. Right into Pete's arms.

5

A CLUE

On Sunday morning, just after daybreak, *The Daily Pilot* skidded to a stop on the Jacksons' driveway. Suzanne raced outside and flipped the paper over before returning to the kitchen. She spread the front page across the breakfast table. *There it is.*

"Wounded man found in deep ravine," read the headline. The subhead added, "Wickenburg resident rescued by Prescott's own mystery searchers." Heidi had done her job, holding back nothing—except one key detail.

"You can't write about the legend of Rattler Mine," Derek had advised the star reporter a day earlier, just before leaving Mr. Wakefield's homestead.

Heidi's button nose twitched. "You're killing me. How can I leave out such a critical part of the story?"

"Mention anything to do with gold," he responded, "and everyone and his dog will be out there searching. It'll turn into a stampede. *That* could destroy potential evidence we haven't yet found *and* provide cover for the perpetrator. We expect he'll be back, nosing around, and we're keeping a sharp eye open. Don't worry, you'll get your story, all right. I'll see to it, and soon too. Be patient." As always, the detective's reasoning made perfect sense.

"The story's all over the Internet too," Sherri reported. "That means it'll be on the local news stations as well."

The Chief nodded. "Yeah, they'll tag onto to Heidi's article. The whole county will soon know about Mr. Wakefield. But no one has a clue what this case is really about: gold and the Rattler Mine. Darn good thing too."

After breakfast, Tom's cellphone buzzed. The Yavapai County Sheriff's Office, Derek informed him, had released Mr. Wakefield's truck and trailer, which had yielded no clues.

"I let Cynthia Myers know as well," the detective said. "She wondered if you would run Sugarcane home. She offered to take care of the horse until Herb's discharge from the hospital."

That was still a question mark. The Brunellis' mother had kept the foursome in the loop. "Mr. Wakefield is suffering the effects of prolonged hypovolemic shock— severe blood loss that prevents the heart from pumping sufficient blood through the body. He received a transfusion as soon as he arrived at the hospital, of course. But his tissues didn't get enough oxygen for hours after he was shot, potentially leading to permanent tissue and organ damage. We don't know yet. He's still unconscious, still in Intensive Care."

AFTER CHURCH AND A CUSTOMARY FAMILY MEXICAN BRUNCH with their parents and the Brunelli family, the Chief dropped the twins off so they could pick up Herb Wakefield's truck and trailer from the county's impound lot. Suzanne drove, making her way out to the Flying W, only to find that the Brunellis had arrived minutes earlier.

The foursome soon made friends with Sugarcane. That wasn't hard to do. She was a gentle beast who took an instant liking to them all.

Rob Rhinehart and his two wranglers, Gary and Frank, ambled over to say hello. "How's that fellow doing, anyway?" Rob asked. He couldn't recall the man's name.

"Herb Wakefield—he's still in a coma at Prescott Regional Medical Center," Kathy replied. "They're not sure if he'll make it or not."

Gary wondered about a break in the case. "Does the sheriff have any idea who shot the guy?"

"No, sir," Tom replied. "Not a clue. It's quite a mystery."

Frank stroked the horse's nose. "I found her a mile away from the ravine. She was busy feasting on the grass out there, but happy to see me. You're a friendly one, aren't you?"

Suzanne led Sugarcane into the trailer. Tom drove, his first experience handling a good-size truck and trailer that had, he reported to his sister, more than two-hundred-thousand miles on the odometer. The tricky part involved negotiating the multiple switchbacks. He positively crawled around the hairpin curves as impatient drivers piled up behind.

That included Pete, following in the Brunellis' Mustang. On average, it was a one-hour jaunt to Wickenburg; the journey stretched into two. "Should we just get out and push?" he complained at the ninety-minute mark.

Kathy giggled. "I'd give anything to see that."

As the vehicles pulled onto Herb's dirt road, Cynthia waved from a beat-up old deck chair outside the cabin. She stood up and made her wait out to the trailer. Sugarcane whinnied when she recognized Cynthia—they were old friends.

"Any news about Herb?" she asked anxiously.

"Still in a coma," Kathy replied, wanting to offer a ray of hope. "My mom said he's moving around in bed a bit more. That's a good sign."

"Thank goodness."

The older woman backed Sugarcane out of the trailer. "We can just let her go. She'll head right to the stable. I'll bet she's hungry and thirsty." Sure enough, Sugarcane knew she had arrived home.

"I've got something for you," Cynthia said. She held out a small piece of irregularly shaped ore that fit into her palm. "I'm positive this is one that Herb showed me—it was about this size and quite valuable, her said." Clusters of golden crystals glittered in a chunk of clear quartz in her hand.

"Oh my gosh," Suzanne said. "Where did you find it?"

"I made coffee this morning while I waited for you. Herb keeps his filters in the metal draw under the oven. When I opened the drawer, it pushed this—this, uh, ore out onto the linoleum floor. I think whoever stole the samples must have dropped it. My guess is that it tumbled underneath the stove, where the perpetrator couldn't find it."

"Or it was too small to mess with," Pete said. He plucked the sample from her hand, surprised at how heavy it felt.

"Whoa," Tom said. "That's actual gold, for sure. We studied that stuff in Boy Scouts. And we toured a couple of old mines back then."

Suzanne nodded. "So did we—remember, Kathy?"

"Uh-huh. But how can you tell one ore sample from another—and figure out where it came from?"

"We need an assayer," Pete said. "And there's bound to be one in Prescott."

6

GOLD!

On Monday morning, the mystery searchers converged on A&M Minerals, just off Marina Street in downtown Prescott. They had Googled on Sunday night to find a local assayer. Walt McLaughlin's name had popped up.

The girls led the way, stepping through the front door of a hundred-year-old single-story building. A bell rang—it sounded like an old-fashioned bicycle bell—as they walked in. The place reeked of stale tobacco smoke. Dozens of floor-to-ceiling narrow shelves lined the small office, covered with ore samples of every shape and size.

A short, thin man with little hair sat behind the counter. He wore glasses that partially hid heavy bags under both eyes. Kathy thought he might be in his early fifties. "Good morning," he said, looking up and greeting them in a friendly tone. "What can I do for you?"

"Are you Mr. McLaughlin?" Suzanne asked.

"Walt," he replied. He had a pleasant smile. "Who do I have the honor of meeting?"

The foursome introduced themselves and shook hands with the man. They knew they had to be careful about what they revealed to him. As Detective Ryan had warned, any rumor of gold on the meadowlands could start a stampede.

"The reason we're here today," Tom explained, "is to get your professional opinion on a piece of ore that came into our possession." He set the ore sample down on the counter.

Walt picked the sample up and scrutinized it through an eyepiece. Silence reigned as his gaze bored into it from every angle. He grunted to himself before glancing up. "Where did this come from?"

"It belongs to a local prospector," Pete answered truthfully.

Walt shook his head in wonder. "I've been an assayer all of my adult life. No one's ever brought in a piece of crystalline gold like this. It's out there, of course. Round Mountain mine in Nevada produced a lot of it back in the day. But there's nothing similar in Arizona, except . . ." His voice trailed off as he picked up the eyeglass once more.

"Except—?" Suzanne prompted.

"Well, here, let me show you something." He slipped from behind the counter and stepped over to the adjacent wall. He reached up to the highest shelf and snagged a piece of ore. Then he turned around and laid it on the countertop.

"See that?" A jagged chunk of shiny gold crystals embedded in quartz glinted back at the foursome. The similarities between the two samples startled them.

"That," he said, jabbing it with his little finger, "is a piece of crystalline gold—'crystal gold' some people call it—that I purchased twenty-five years ago. I paid four hundred bucks for it at a trade show in Las Vegas. Supposedly, it came from Rattler Mine, rumored to be a gold-rich cave beside a stream somewhere out north of Prescott. Lost, according to legend, in the eighteen-eighties."

He leaned closer to the foursome, almost as if he were sharing a secret. His voice dropped an octave, and his eyes grew larger. "But no one really knows. Not for sure. Today, this sample is worth six grand, maybe more."

The mystery searchers didn't show their reaction, but their minds raced. *Rattler Mine... "It's there... I found it..."*

Pete inhaled sharply. "*Six grand.* You mean to say that—"

"That your piece is worth that much?" the man finished. "Yup, and even more. Here's why. What makes crystalline gold so valuable is not just its high gold and silver content—there's twenty percent silver in my sample—but also its natural beauty. What you brought in is classic crystalline gold, and collectors love the stuff. The value can be many times greater than the market price of the amount of metal in it. Instead of being melted down into bullion, fine specimens like this one are collected and displayed like gemstones, or made into jewelry."

"What I'm curious about," Walt said, his eyes narrowing as he surveyed the foursome, "is where your friend found this. Today, they still find this type of crystalline gold in California, Nevada, and Colorado mines. But if he discovered this one in Arizona, he may have stumbled across that legendary old Rattler Mine. And if he did, well..."

7

A NEW ASSIGNMENT

That afternoon, the mystery searchers and Heidi Hoover met Derek at the Shake Shack, their favorite meeting place since junior high.

Pete—the one with a prodigious appetite—was chomping down a double-double burger as the detective pulled into the parking lot.

"That stuff's bad for you," Kathy chided her brother.

He ignored the dig and kept right on eating. *"Mmm—mm, so good."* He licked his fingers with a slurping sound, much to his sister's disdain.

Derek parked his unmarked cruiser and ordered a coffee before making his way to the outside picnic table. He sat down and pulled out a little notebook from his shirt pocket. "Well, I have a couple of interesting items for you." He took a sip of the bitter brew.

"Tell us," Suzanne said.

"I've run background checks on a few people: Rob Rhinehart, Gary Brown, Frank Hanson, and Cynthia Myers. Guess who has a prison record?"

Pete said, "Frank Hanson."

"Gary Brown," Kathy reckoned.

"Nope. Cynthia Myers."

Eyebrows rose around the table.

"Cynthia!" Suzanne exclaimed. "For what, and when?"

"Forty years ago, they sentenced her to five-to-fifteen for embezzlement," the detective read from his notes. "Money disappeared from a Colorado bank that employed her. She served five years in a federal lockup before being released on good behavior. Then she moved to Wickenburg and has been clean ever since."

Suzanne shook her head. "And still is, I bet. She had nothing to do with this."

"Why not?" Pete said.

"Well, for one thing, she doesn't own a horse. Whoever shot Mr. Wakefield had to ride in there with him, or following him. And she told us she can't tell one piece of ore from another."

Pete said, "We don't know that . . . not for sure."

"We don't know anything for sure," Kathy argued. "But it seemed rather obvious to me she was telling the truth."

In Suzanne's mind likewise, Cynthia had passed the character test. "Remember when she fainted at Mr. Wakefield's? That wasn't an act, it was for real. She's lucky she didn't break her hip on the way down."

"Pete broke her fall," Kathy said. "Good catch, bro."

He grinned at the rare compliment. The siblings sparred regularly, but they cared for one another. A lot.

"Everyone else's record was clean?" Tom asked.

Derek nodded. "For sure. Nothing for Gary at all. Frank has picked up a few speeding tickets in his day. That's it. And the sheriff has known Rob Rhinehart all his life. They grew up together."

"I can't imagine Mr. Rhinehart hurting anyone, it's true," said Tom. "And his ranch hands sure seem like nice guys. But having no prior record doesn't mean either one of them couldn't be the culprit. They're out riding in the grasslands all the time—"

His sister picked up the thread. "So they could have seen Mr. Wakefield out prospecting, kept an eye on him—"

"Waiting for him to reveal the location of a strike . . ." Kathy added.

"Maybe so," Derek said. "But we have zero evidence for that so far."

A long moment passed in glum silence.

"So where do we go now?" Pete asked.

"Nowhere," Derek replied. "I agree with the sentiment expressed here. In my mind, Cynthia is likely innocent. She made a mistake but paid the price and moved on."

"Agreed," Suzanne said. "What else?"

"What time did you find Wakefield in the ravine?"

The mystery searchers glanced at one another. "Around two in the afternoon," Kathy replied.

"Uh-huh." Derek looked away for a few seconds. "About then, Wakefield's cellphone pinged a cell tower—seven miles north of Prescott on Highway 89."

Pete's eyes widened. "Interesting."

"Right. It pinged again, inside the city limits, ten minutes later. Then, nothing."

"So that's when the perp shut off Mr. Wakefield's cell," Tom concluded. Growing up in the Chief's household, the twins had learned that *perp* was police slang for *perpetrator*— they loved to use police jargon.

"Or when he destroyed it," Kathy said. "One or the other."

Suzanne added it up. "So Mr. Wakefield fell to the bottom of the ravine about an hour before we found him. It would take that long for the assailant to ride back to Highway 89, where Mr. Wakefield's stolen phone pinged the first cell tower."

"Or someone pushed him," Pete said. "Kinda explains the loss of blood—lying there for so long."

Kathy hated the sticky stuff. The thought of it made her gag.

"Now it's our turn, Derek," Tom said, glancing over to the red-haired detective. He pulled out the piece of ore and laid it in front of him. The foursome explained how Cynthia had found the sample. And what they had learned at A&M Assayers.

Derek picked it up, bouncing the ore in one hand. "Heavy, isn't it?"

"Uh-huh," Suzanne said. "It's gold and quartz, and both have a good natural weight to them."

"And this is a sample from Mr. Wakefield's kitchen table?"

Tom nodded. "Cynthia thinks so."

"What's it worth?"

"Six grand, maybe more," Pete said, waving a hand as if that were nothing.

The detective let out a low whistle. "The day I visited his cabin, there were about ten pieces of ore lined up on his kitchen table. They looked like this one, some were larger. They all had these same clusters of gold crystals embedded in quartz. I figured it for fool's gold. I mean, who would leave valuable ore on the kitchen table? If your assayer is right, someone made off with more than fifty grand in gold. *Wow*."

"How did the shooter find out about Rattler Mine?" Kathy wondered out loud.

"Good question," Derek replied. "We probably won't discover the answer unless Wakefield recovers. Which brings me to the next issue. Right now, I have a problem—I need your help."

"Sure," Tom said. "What can we do?"

The detective sipped his cooling coffee. "Herb Wakefield is still in a coma. A couple of things will happen if he regains consciousness."

"He'll identify his assailant, and you'll arrest him," Suzanne said.

"Well, I hope so—" Derek said, chuckling.

"Maybe not," Pete said. "Someone shot Mr. Wakefield in the back. It's possible he never even saw the shooter."

"Right you are," Derek replied. "Anyway, Wakefield will lay claim to Rattler Mine—"

"But whoever shot him," Suzanne put in, "doesn't want that to happen."

"Correct," Derek concluded.

"*W-wait a sec,*" Pete said. "You mean that—"

"Someone might try to do him in," Kathy said, finishing his thought. "Even in the hospital . . ."

"That's exactly what I mean," Detective Robinson said calmly. "Whoever shot him wouldn't have any problem finishing the job. In fact, they might feel they have little choice. If Wakefield survives, the perpetrator could end up with free room and board at Florence State Prison. Probably for a nice long stretch."

"Whoever that person is must know that Mr. Wakefield is still alive," Suzanne said. "Heidi's story got a lot of coverage."

"And *where* he is," Kathy added. "There's only one major hospital in Prescott with an intensive care unit."

"Is the Sheriff's Office guarding him around the clock?" Tom asked.

"Uh-huh. I've got a deputy parked outside his door right now. We've been watching Mr. Wakefield ever since he arrived in Emergency. But this is the summer season, and we're swamped. The sheriff wants every deputy on the street. I was hoping you'd be willing to monitor the gentleman."

"You mean, like, watch him? At the hospital?" Kathy hated stakeouts.

"Right. Just hang in with him, sit outside his room. Make sure only medical people gain access. If the perp makes it in and notices a guard, no way will he try to take Wakefield out."

"Deal," Pete said, hiding a grin. Another stakeout. Unlike his sister, he loved them.

"Okay," Tom said, noting the expression on Suzanne's face. She was all in. "We can do that. Starting when?"

"Today, at four o'clock. Take turns. Anyone spot anything suspicious, dial nine-one-one and hospital security. Then call me."

8

THE STAKEOUT

The mystery searchers settled on six-hour shifts. They drew lots to see who would cover them, and when. Before drawing the first card, Kathy blinked and asked, "Is ace high or low?"

"Who cares?" Pete smirked. "You won't get one, anyway."

"High," Tom said.

She pulled up an ace and taunted her brother with a devilish grin. "I'll take the four-to-ten p.m. shift today."

Suzanne flipped over a king. "Ten until four a.m."

Now the pick of the next shifts was between the two boys. Pete drew first and stared at his deuce in disbelief. "Dang it."

Tom won with a six and stifled a smile. "I'll take ten o'clock tomorrow morning."

Pete groaned. "Four a.m.? *Pitiful.*"

Kathy arrived at the hospital a few minutes early. She searched for her mom in the Emergency unit and said a quick hello before stepping into an open elevator. The ride came to a smooth stop on the second floor, its doors opening with a *whoosh* into Intensive Care.

She stepped into a familiar marble-lined hallway lit with harsh fluorescent lighting and animated with a steady murmur of hushed voices. The usual antiseptic, bleach-like smell assaulted her nostrils. Somewhere down the hall, low-volume monitors played television comedies with frequent bursts of quiet laughter—the family rooms—punctuating the continuous background of soft electronic bleeps and blips.

At the nurse's station—always the ward's hub of activity —a short distance to her left, Kathy recognized Nurse Gloria Hernandez, a friend of her mother's. She made her way over and exchanged a few words.

"Kathy!" Gloria exclaimed, giving her a hug. "How are you?" She wore blue scrubs and a big smile. "Are you looking for your mom?"

"Hi, Mrs. Hernandez," Kathy replied. "No, I just said hello to her in Emergency. I'm here to relieve the deputy watching Mr. Wakefield."

"Oh, mystery searchers stuff, huh?" Gloria said, suddenly looking very serious. "We're expecting you. The police told us you'd be helping out. The deputy is just around the corner. You can't miss her."

Kathy found Deputy Angela Harper sitting in a folding chair outside room 211, checking her cellphone. The two had met before on the Sidewinder Lane mystery.

The deputy stood and shook hands with her. "It's Kathy, right? Sorry you're the one who has to take over. You'll be bored silly before this is over."

"I get it," Kathy said with a half-smile. "I've done stakeouts before. They're usually far from exciting."

Deputy Harper agreed. "That's a fact. Long and boring

would be my take. I'll be back on patrol, thankfully. Hang in here for a sec. I'll call hospital security and introduce you."

A minute later, a young, uniformed man named Edward Statler—tall and slim, with black, slicked-back hair—rounded the corner and held out his hand.

"I've briefed Mr. Statler on the schedule," the deputy said as she introduced the two. "He knows your role is to make sure that only medical personnel enter the room. No one else."

Edward pointed to a corner camera near the ceiling. "I doubt anyone could get this far. But if you see a stranger who isn't a medical person, just dial zero-one-one on the nurse's desk phone. That goes directly to security."

"Got it."

"Call me if you need anything. If you want a break, dial us and we'll take over. Our instructions are that someone is outside this room at all times."

Soon enough, Deputy Harper said her goodbyes, and Edward headed back to the security station.

Kathy had brought a turkey sandwich, one Granny Smith apple, and plenty of bottled water. She had also lugged in something to read—an exploration novel. Over the next few hours, she fairly flew through the entire book. *Excellent.* At various times she greeted the same four nurses dressed in green or blue scrubs who worked the floor, but they didn't have time to chat. Gloria had finished her shift earlier.

Kathy got to her feet often and walked in circles close to the room. At one point, she realized the never-ending electronic bleeps and blips had faded deeper into the background. *I'm just getting used to them,* she thought.

Once she peeked into Mr. Wakefield's semi dark room. She recognized the bushy red beard. The patient lay on his back, his upper body raised at a slight angle, eyes closed, chest rising and falling, covered by a thin sheet. Half a dozen tubes ran around his body, and several monitors encircled him, each one creating its own unique sound.

It had been three days since they had found Mr. Wakefield. "Still touch and go," Maria had reported earlier. Kathy said a silent prayer for him.

An hour passed before Suzanne walked up and startled her. "Hey, you! What's happening?"

"Hey, yourself. Not a thing. Quiet as a mouse. I'll make a call and introduce you to security."

TIME DRAGGED ON THE HOSPITAL WARD. AFTER MIDNIGHT, IT seemed to pass even more slowly. Suzanne's eyes felt heavier with every passing hour.

Often, she'd stand up and do exercises in the empty hallway. Twice, she wandered over to the nurse's station and chatted with the duty nurses when they didn't seem too busy. One of them—Wendi—had graduated from Prescott High six years earlier. It was quiet for her too.

Drinking from her water bottle helped. Suzanne refilled it from the fountain. Reading *didn't* help—in fact, it made her even sleepier.

Every hour, a nurse stepped into Mr. Wakefield's room to check on his vitals. Suzanne surveyed the shadowy room from the doorway while the nurse was at work. The sounds reverberating in the hallway intensified inside Mr. Wakefield's room. A hushed cacophony of bleeps and blips emerged from the multiple electronic devices monitoring him and, she figured, keeping the poor man alive.

As the nurse gently closed the door to Mr. Wakefield's room after her fifth visit, Suzanne slipped back to her chair and sat down again. A glance at her cellphone showed 3:54

a.m. Pete, she knew, would be along any minute. The nurse returned to her station before heading out to another patient's room.

A few seconds later, Suzanne heard an alarm—*beep, beep, beep!*—ringing out from the nurses' station. A nurse shouted out and began racing up the hallway. Suzanne sprang from her seat, grabbed the door to Mr. Wakefield's room and yanked it.

Wait!

The window was open. Out of the corner of one eye, Suzanne saw—*something*—moving—

Then everything went dark.

9

EVIDENCE

"No one's ever tried to bump off one of our patients," a flustered Dr. Truegood said.

The doctor—bald, middle-aged, wearing a stiff white jacket, with a stethoscope draped around his neck—stood in the hallway outside Mr. Wakefield's room. The silent corridor had erupted into a noisy impromptu gathering of police, medical personnel, and security. Not to mention the mystery searchers.

And people kept coming—including Heidi Hoover. "Oh, my gosh, Suzanne. Are you *okay?*"

"Define okay," she quipped, touching the crown of her head. "Yeah, I'm fine, Heidi. Thanks for asking."

Pete had arrived for his shift just as hospital security raced over to Mr. Wakefield's room. After checking on Suzanne, he punched out a series of calls. The Chief ran Tom over in his unmarked cruiser, picking up Kathy on the way. They pulled in at the same time as Derek Robinson. Sheriff McClennan was close behind.

Derek had two immediate questions. "How did the

intruder know which room to hit? And, how did he find it from outside the building?"

"That's easy," Dr. Truegood explained. "If the perpetrator called the front desk and pretended to be a close family member asking about visiting hours, they'd provide the room number. And there's a floor plan with room numbers on the hospital website."

The sheriff groaned. "Well, there you go."

"It'd be a good idea to delete that floor plan," the Chief growled. He wasn't overjoyed. For one thing, his only daughter had come too close to a dangerous criminal. For another, it was four-thirty in the morning. There would be problems when they returned home. Sherri wouldn't like this. Not at all.

"Mr. Wakefield needs to change rooms," the sheriff ordered.

"I'll handle it right away," the doctor said.

"And the Sheriff's Office will take over guarding Mr. Wakefield," Derek informed everyone. "Whoever this guy is, he's way too dangerous."

"You never saw or heard anything?" the Chief asked, meeting Suzanne's gaze. She held a bag of ice on top of her head.

"Well, I figured *something* was wrong. It had suddenly grown quieter, and I couldn't figure out why. Then that alarm rang on the nursing station and Wendi"—she nodded to the nurse standing beside her—"started running toward me. I raced into the room. The last thing I remember is seeing an open window. When I opened my eyes, Dr. True-good and two nurses were looking straight down at me. I realized someone had conked me a good one."

"You were very lucky it wasn't worse," the Chief said, still glowering.

"I came along a minute later," Pete explained. "By then it was all over. Suzanne was coming out of it. So Dan and I"—he pointed to a tall young guy in a private security company uniform—"raced down into the parking lot, but there wasn't a soul around."

Tom asked, "Dan, does the hospital have surveillance cameras out there?"

"For sure," he replied. "We already checked the video before and after the incursion. There was no suspicious activity."

"So that means the perp didn't drive in?" Heidi wondered out loud.

"Correct," Dan said. "He had to have walked over."

The Chief addressed the nurse. "What did you see?"

The mystery searchers and Heidi stood by, taking in every word.

Wendi blinked as she gathered her thoughts. "I was seconds behind Suzanne, but when I rushed through the door, she was already lying flat on her back. At the same moment, I spotted a woman slipping out the window."

"A woman," the sheriff said. "Are you sure?"

"It all happened so fast but, yes. She appeared to be slim, not tall, with longish grey hair. I only saw her from the back. And to be honest, I focused more on Suzanne and Mr. Wakefield—they both needed help. I treated Suzanne while the other nurses plugged all the systems back in. Whoever this person was, she pulled the plugs on everything and ripped out all the tubes."

"But Mr. Wakefield is okay?" Kathy asked.

"He's fine," Dr. Truegood answered. "The interruption was brief, and we only have him on hydration, nutrition, and meds. No life support. The guy's a tough old bird. I'm hoping he'll pull through."

The door to room 211 opened. Two crime scene technicians stepped out, tool kits in hand. One of them carried a transparent plastic evidence bag.

"Not a single print on the glass windows," she reported. "And they keep the interior squeaky clean, so nothing there either. But the tree outside snagged a little souvenir from her—the assailant I mean."

"'Her,' huh," Sheriff McClennan repeated. "What is it?"

"It's a tissue with lipstick on it," the tech said.

"A woman, you're *sure*?" Heidi asked, skeptically.

"Well, someone left the tissue behind," the technician replied. "Whether it was a male or female remains to be seen." She grinned at the detective. "That's your job."

"How did she climb up to the second floor?" Tom asked.

"Oak tree," Pete said. "Dan pointed it out from the parking lot. It's an easy climb."

"Any security cameras on that side of the hospital?" Pete asked.

"Negative," Dan replied. "There's no door there. At every entrance there are cameras, yes, and covering the parking lot too. But nothing monitors the outside walls. No one ever anticipated people climbing trees to break in to the hospital."

"Now we know better," Suzanne said ruefully. Her head began to pound. "Wouldn't the intruder realize that an alarm would sound if she unplugged stuff?"

The sheriff grunted. "You'd sure think so."

LATER THAT MORNING, AFTER CATCHING UP ON THEIR SLEEP, the mystery searchers connected with Derek on a conference call. Even over the phone, he sounded tired.

"You didn't catch some shut-eye?" Kathy asked.

"No such luck," he replied wryly. "I've been hammering

away at two other cases since our excitement in the early hours. You feeling okay, Suzanne?"

"I am. Head's still sore, no big deal," she replied.

"The 'big deal' happened when we arrived home," Tom related. "Mom wasn't too happy."

"I'll bet not," the detective chuckled. "I think we'd better keep you guys off the firing line."

"No way, Derek," Pete objected. "Suzanne's fine. We're all on the case. Lead on!"

Laughter rang out on both sides of the line. "Okay," Derek said, "but let's keep our heads down. Whoever the perp is, she's dangerous."

"We've only run into one woman so far who could be a suspect," Tom noted.

Kathy arched her eyebrows. "Can you imagine Cynthia Myers climbing a tree and bonking Suzanne on the head? I sure can't."

"Neither can I," Suzanne said, touching the crown of her head. *Ouch.* "She's slender and looks pretty fit, but she moves slowly."

"Plus, Cynthia's hair is white and cut short," Tom said. "The assailant's is long and grey."

"Could be a wig," said Pete. "A disguise."

"I agree with the ladies here," Derek said. "I don't see Cynthia climbing that tree up to the second floor."

"That's a fact," Heidi said. "She'd fall down and break her neck."

Pete spoke up, rather impatiently. It bugged him that no one had a clue. "So who is this woman, anyway?"

"Whoever she is," Derek replied, "we have yet to run into her. But we will. It's only a matter of time. Meantime, I'm going to drive out to Wickenburg after lunch and interview Cynthia once more. Anyone want to come with me?"

Suzanne and Kathy glanced at each other. "We will," they chimed almost in unison.

"I can't," Heidi said. "Too much on my plate."

"What about you guys?" the detective asked the boys. "Any plans?"

Tom had a ready answer. "We're going horseback riding."

"Dude!" Pete cheered, exchanging a high-five with his best friend.

10

PUZZLE PIECES

Cynthia Myers took the news of the assault on her friend's life in stride. And her face expressed relief when she heard about the minimal harm done to Suzanne.

"Thank goodness," she said. "And yes, that sounds like Rosemary. The grey in her hair is premature. I've never met her, but Herb described her to me. She was just another person he tried to help." She rolled her eyes in wonder. "One of many."

The girls had accompanied Derek to Wickenburg. Arriving right after 2:00 p.m., they turned down the same gravel road toward Mr. Wakefield's acreage. A quarter mile in, not far from Mr. Wakefield's driveway, the detective pulled a left turn into a small homesite. At the end of a dirt track stood a single-wide manufactured home. Cynthia sat beside a round patio table out front, waiting.

Derek came to a stop beside her SUV. The three stepped out and joined her around the table.

Cynthia offered cold lemonade from a pitcher chock-full

of ice cubes. The four of them chatted a bit about Mr. Wakefield's condition before Derek got down to business.

"Do you recall Rosemary's last name?" he asked.

"Nope. Herb never mentioned it. But she called him a few times, looking for help."

"How old would she be?" Suzanne asked.

"He figured she might be in her late thirties, but she had a few problems. He told me they weighed on her, aging her before her time."

"What kind of problems?"

"He didn't say."

"Where did he meet her?" Kathy asked.

"On Courthouse Square, across from Whiskey Row. She hadn't eaten that day, so Herb bought her lunch. He always had a big heart. He gave her some cash too."

"Okay," Derek said, nodding. "Anything else about her appearance? Race or ethnicity?"

"Native American. From south of the border, he told me."

Suzanne asked, "Does Mr. Wakefield have any family or friends?"

"Me. That's it. He's kept to himself, socially, for as long as I've known him. Once, years ago, he talked a little about his parents. He was an only child and hailed from Prescott. Nothing else."

"But he helped people," Tom said.

"All the time. But they didn't become his *friends*. They were more like his projects. I think Herb had experienced tough times when he was younger. He'd give a stranger the shirt off his back. He just had a lot of compassion built into him."

. . .

MEANWHILE, THE BOYS DROVE OUT TO THE FLYING W DUDE Ranch. They had called Rob Rhinehart earlier and asked to borrow a couple of horses. "Sure, no problem," he had said. "Tell me what you're up to when you get here."

The boys met Rob outside his big barn. "Pete, you ride Trigger, and Tom, you take—what do you call her?—'Goldie.' You each built a good relationship with your horse during your week here. Might as well take advantage of that. So, where ya goin'?"

"We'd like to circle the area where we found Mr. Wakefield," Tom replied. "We still haven't figured out how he ended up in that ravine."

"And check out some of the old mines," Pete added.

"Well, you're heading off into a thousand acres," Rob said. "There's a passel of closed claims out there. We capped the shafts that go straight down—don't want anyone falling in one of 'em. Prospectors tunneled others into the sides of hills and rock formations. You can walk in, but watch out for snakes."

"Count on it," Pete said.

"A few hundred yards northeast of that ravine is a watering hole—an oasis. Ride the horses over there and let them drink."

"Got it," Pete said. "We're still looking for leads on whoever's trying to bump off Herb Wakefield. Someone attacked him again on Sunday."

"You gotta be kidding me!" Rob said. "The guy tried to get him—in the *hospital?*"

"The police think it was a woman," Tom said. He explained about the trace of lipstick and the nurse's eyewitness account. "She made it right into Mr. Wakefield's room and pulled out all his tubes and monitor wires and stuff, but her plan didn't work out. The nurses hooked him up again in minutes, but the intruder got away."

"Now I've heard everything," Rob muttered. "Okay. Off you go. Ride safely."

Trigger recognized Pete and whinnied at the sight of him. Excited to ride once more, Pete set the saddle blanket and saddle in place, cinched up the girth around Trigger's ribcage, inserted the bit into the horse's mouth, and secured the bridle on his head. He led Trigger out of the barn and mounted on the left side, placing his foot in the stirrup and pulling himself up. Just as the wranglers had taught them.

It turned out that 'Goldie' was out on a ride, so Tom chose Suzanne's strawberry roan. He filled a saddlebag with snacks, water, and a flashlight, then hurried to catch up to his best friend.

"Which way?" Pete asked.

"Let's head due north. We'll use the ravine where we found Herb as a starting point."

Dark and threatening overcast clouds had replaced the brilliant blue skies from a day earlier. Thunder rumbled in the distance.

Pete craned his neck around. "We might be in for it."

The boys followed a familiar route that, for the most part, appeared untouched by humans. Still, every so often they crossed an old mining road, more like a trail, really— stamped into the terrain a century earlier. They wound their way toward long forgotten claims and capped mine shafts that they imagined plunging straight down into the earth. Once they dismounted and pried open one of the wooden caps. Pete dropped a small rock into the abyss. A few seconds slipped past before the sound of a quiet splash echoed back.

"There's water down there!" Tom exclaimed. "A *long* way down." That thought had not crossed their minds. But of course groundwater, they realized, would seep into an abandoned mineshaft.

Later—just before reaching the ravine—they explored a five-foot-wide tunnel cut horizontally into a rocky formation. Tom led the way into a shaft that was over six feet high, painting a path of light along the rocky floor for a few yards before they came to an abrupt end. An eerie feeling passed over them as they ran their hands over a chipped wall of solid rock.

"Bet no one has touched this in a hundred years," Pete said.

"Longer, I'd guess," Tom said. "Add another half a century. Gold mining started in Arizona in the eighteen-sixties. Weird, isn't it?" Their voices sounded dead in the surrounding space.

"Imagine digging this by hand . . . with a *pick*," Pete said. "Then giving up and moving to a new site."

"Wow."

Soon, they paused on the edge of the ravine where their adventure had begun. Tom dug a canteen out of his saddlebag. They each gulped down a couple of slugs of water. "Okay. Let's water the horses and check out the area."

A few hundred yards away, forty-foot-high weeping willows poked up from the sides of a bowl-like oasis that sloped downward from the surrounding meadowlands. The boys rode over and followed a narrow, well-traveled trail that angled down to the waterhole. The horses handled the slope with ease.

"They've been here before," Pete said.

"Yup," Tom said. "It's old home week for them." They dismounted and allowed the horses to drink to their hearts' content.

Pete bent over and stared hard at the soft, muddy ground that surrounded the pond. "Tom, check it out."

"What is it?"

"Remember the distinct horseshoe with that bent nailhead?"

Tom leaned closer. "You're kidding, right?"

"Nope. Look! Hoofprints all over the place, and you can't miss that one. Whoever rode in here didn't dismount, which is too bad. We'd have the rider's footprints too. The mud is still pliable. This horse watered out here yesterday or—"

"Or even this morning," Tom cut in. He straightened up, looking around warily. "You know what this means?"

"Sure. He—or she—is searching for Rattler Mine. And doesn't have a clue where it is, any more than we do. Yet."

Just then, the skies opened up.

11

SURPRISE!

On Wednesday morning, the twins caught up with their parents at breakfast. The Chief hadn't arrived home until late the previous night. Now, the recent events spilled out over eggs and coffee.

For Suzanne, missing out on a horseback ride was a big deal. "Tom had all the fun," she groused.

Her brother tried to mollify his sister. "You and Kathy got to head over to Wickenburg with Derek Robinson."

She rolled her eyes. "Oh, joy."

The Chief laughed. He encouraged the twins' ambitions at every opportunity. "Hey, police work can be boring. Better get used to do it." He often said law enforcement was ninety-nine percent pure boredom and one percent sheer terror.

"We spent most of the time in a car," Suzanne moaned.

"Yup. That's what officers do. I put in my fair share too. What did you learn?"

"Not much. We got a lead on a lady named Rosemary. She hangs around Courthouse Square and has prematurely grey hair."

"That's interesting," Sherri said. "So did the intruder at the hospital, you said. But I thought Mr. Wakefield was a loner."

"Except when it comes to rescuing people," Suzanne explained. "When he found Rosemary, she hadn't eaten all day. It appears he bought her lunch and kept in touch after that."

Sherri liked that. "He must be a caring individual."

"What about you, Tom?" the Chief asked.

"We borrowed horses from the Flying W and checked out the land near the ravine. Remember that distinctive hoofprint with the bent nailhead? We spotted the same horse's prints at the nearby watering hole. And they were fresh."

"How fresh?"

"Early this morning, or late yesterday, I estimate. The mud was still wet and gooey."

"Well, that *is* interesting. I'd bet anything the rider is searching for Rattler Mine."

"That's what we figured," Tom said.

"I'll bet you're right," Suzanne said.

"What's your next move?" the Chief asked.

"Those meadowlands are endless," Tom replied. "You could ride for days and never see a soul. I think we'll run a drone out there this afternoon. We'll never discover the mine from the air, but we could spot a rider."

"Good idea. You'll cover a lot of ground, and fast. What about you, Suzie?"

"Me?" she replied, perking up. "I'm going with Tom. The Brunellis can look for Rosemary."

AN HOUR LATER, PETE AND KATHY RENDEZVOUSED WITH Derek in downtown Prescott. They parked their cars side by side on Whiskey Row, strolled across the street, and circled all four sides of Courthouse Square. No luck.

Small groups of people were enjoying the verdant green lawns that surrounded the historic Yavapai County Courthouse. Children played and shrieked, dog walkers crisscrossed the park, and couples relaxed on benches. But nobody came close to matching Rosemary's description.

"Let's cross over to Gurley Street and grab some coffee," Derek suggested.

"Good idea," Pete replied. "I'm hungry."

Kathy poked him. "What's new?"

They found outside tables and chairs and sat down at one that offered a wide view of Courthouse Square. Pete enjoyed a humongous pecan roll. The lady didn't show. Half an hour later, Derek's cellphone buzzed with an incoming message.

"Sorry, gotta run," he said. "Hang around as long as you can. I'll circle back when I can."

RIGHT AFTER THE CHIEF HAD HEADED OFF TO WORK, THE twins called Ray Huntley, president of Prescott High's technology club,

"Ray, can we borrow the drone?" Tom asked. The compact, lightweight flying machine had been essential in unraveling a few of the mystery searchers' previous cases. Ray had never turned them down, and today was no exception. He knew the foursome always took excellent care of the school's high-tech hardware.

"Sure. Are you working on another mystery?"

"We sure are," Suzanne replied. "Did you read about the prospector we found at the bottom of a ravine?"

"Did I ever. How's he doing?"

After they had picked up the equipment and filled Ray in

a bit more, the twins headed out into the meadowlands. Suzanne drove. They knew that countless old gold-mining trails crisscrossed the area, and that many of them intersected with Highway 89. Sure enough, they had driven only a few miles north before they spotted a promising dirt track leading westward.

"Let's check it out, Suzie."

It showed evidence of recent use—"Off-roaders," Tom guessed. The trail—pitted with huge potholes—forced Suzanne to twist and turn the Chevy with care, skirting the hazards as best she could.

"If we fall into one of those, we'll never get out," she muttered as the car jolted along. Tom hung on for dear life.

Two miles in, the rocky trail dropped into a dry gorge and vanished without a trace. Tom figured a flash flood had washed it away in the distant past. Fortunately, they found themselves protected by soaring rock walls.

"Perfect," Tom exclaimed. "Park right here."

"Why not?" Suzanne agreed. "No one can see us. And there's nowhere to go, except back." The twins stepped out into a cool summer late morning, with a bright blue sky and a gentle breeze that filtered through the gorge. Yesterday's thunderstorm had moved eastward into New Mexico.

"Perfect flying weather," Suzanne said. They pulled out two cases from the Chevy's trunk, both marked FRAGILE—HANDLE WITH CARE, setting them down beside the car. Then they unpacked a handheld controller, extra battery, and the drone itself.

Airtime was thirty minutes, after which the "bird" would require a battery change. "That'll put us out of business for a bit," Tom said. "No big deal." The mystery searchers had plenty of experience flying the sophisticated machine. Tom had served as team leader when Prescott High's technology club built and customized their first drone from a kit.

With a familiar whirring sound—it always reminded the twins of an angry beehive—the aircraft lifted and soared away. Suzanne guided the drone upward reflexively close to four hundred feet, the highest permitted altitude—a limit set by federal law intended to prevent drones from interfering with other aircraft.

"Altitude's no big deal out here, anyway," Suzanne said. "We'll spot mule deer, coyotes, skunks, and elk—but I don't think we're likely to run into any planes or helicopters."

The onboard HD camera captured a live video stream. As she operated the controller, Suzanne could see everything on her screen.

Tom monitored and recorded the view too, from an app on his cell phone. "Okay, camera's live, image is sharp, it's looking good."

"Where to?"

"Depends. Can you figure out the ravine's location?"

"Uh . . . well, yeah, I think so," Suzanne replied. "We should be close. A mile or two northwest."

The view from the air differed dramatically from that at ground level. The passing scenes confused them initially. "I'll fly south until I recognize something," Suzanne said, "then turn around and approach it that way."

Sure enough, that worked. The ravine soon appeared on their screens. *"Whew,"* Suzanne breathed. "That was close. We've only got seven minutes of airtime left. I'll circle around for a bit."

"Okay," Tom said. "Then bring her home for a battery change." The oasis passed below, the water glinting from the overhead view. Grassy meadowlands, rocky ravines, and canyons rushed past, one following the other. The four-hundred-foot level provided a wide-angle panorama.

"We're all alone out here," Suzanne said.

No sooner had she spoken when sharp reports from five rifle shots rang out, one after another. *Bang! Bang! Bang! Bang! . . . Bang!* Loud, clear—and way too close.

"Oh—my—gosh!" Suzanne exclaimed.

"They're after the drone!" Tom shouted. "Bring it home! We gotta get it outta here!"

For some reason, her father's words popped into Suzanne's mind: *"Police work is ninety-nine percent pure boredom and one percent sheer terror."*

"Too late!" she cried. *Terror time.*

12

REVELATIONS

Kathy used her smartwatch to figure out that circling Courthouse Square twenty-two times would equal a five-mile hike. She loved staying in shape with exercise. Plus, time would zip past as they waited for Rosemary to show. *Or not.*

"Let's go," she encouraged her brother.

An hour later, just as they began the eleventh round, Pete spotted someone who matched Rosemary's minimal description. A woman with shoulder-length grey hair had appeared on the courthouse lawn.

"Whaddaya think, Kathy?"

The woman rested on the grass, both arms clutching her knees. Cynthia was right. She looked to be of Native American heritage, and close to forty years old. She wore dirty jeans, running shoes, and a clean short-sleeved blouse.

Suspicious eyes turned their way as Kathy approached, inquiring, "Are you Rosemary?"

"Who's asking?"

"My name is Kathy, and this is my brother, Pete. Do you know a Mr. Herbert Wakefield?"

A half-smile crossed the woman's face. "You mean Herb? Sure, I know him. But I think he's been avoiding me for the last few days."

"He hasn't been avoiding you. He's in the hospital," Pete said.

The woman froze, glancing back and forth between the two. Seconds passed before she found her voice again. "In the hospital . . . what for?"

"Someone shot him out in mining country," Kathy said. "He's in Prescott Regional."

"That explains why he isn't answering his messages," the woman said. She teared up. "Are you friends of his?"

"Four of us found him at the bottom of a ravine," Pete replied. "Now we're working with the Sheriff's Office to find out why someone would want to shoot him."

"So you are Rosemary?" Kathy asked gently.

Rosemary nodded, swallowing hard. "That is so sad. Herb's the nicest guy in the world. He helped me out and I owe him. Is there anything I can do? Can I visit him in the hospital?"

The Brunellis sat down on the grass. "They don't allow visitors in Intensive Care, except close family," Kathy said. She was careful not to mention the late-night intruder. "But you can help by answering a few questions."

No hesitation. "Fire away."

"Do you have a horse?"

Rosemary burst into laughter. "Honey, I don't own anything. And the last thing I'd ever want is a horse. I don't even like them."

Pete asked, "Do you have a driver's license?"

"Nope. Long gone. No car, either."

"Where do you live?"

"Here, there, and everywhere. Herb checked me into a motel for a bit a while back so I could get cleaned up. But today I'm back on the street."

"Did Mr. Wakefield—Herb—tell you what he did for a living?"

"Sort of. He said something about being a prospector. That he'd been at it for a quarter century. To be honest, I didn't think it looked too profitable."

"Did he mention other people to you? Anyone else in his life?" Kathy asked.

"Uh-huh. He has a girlfriend in Wickenburg."

"A girlfriend. Did he call her that?"

"Yup. Cindy or Cynthia, something like that. I never met her."

"When did you last visit Wickenburg?"

"How about never?"

Kathy was just about to ask if Herb had said or done anything unusual the last time Rosemary had seen him when Derek showed up. After Pete and Kathy had introduced her, she clammed up in front of the police officer.

No matter. It had become obvious that—even with her prematurely grey hair—she had nothing to do with shooting Herb Wakefield, nor with his attack in the hospital.

They said goodbye. Derek slipped her a few dollars and thanked her.

"Hey, I appreciate that," Rosemary said. She appeared to see him in a new light. "Breakfast is coming up. Do me a favor. Look me up when I can visit Herb. I owe that man big time."

· · ·

THE TWINS GAPED AT THEIR SCREENS AS THE DRONE cartwheeled toward the ground. Scenes of sky, ground, and rocky ravines twisted and turned for a few seconds as the earth grew closer. Then, nothing.

"He got the bird," Tom groaned.

"Forget that," Suzanne said. "We gotta get out of here."

They tossed everything into the back of the Chevy. Tom leaped into the driver's seat and fired up the ignition. As Suzanne jumped in, Tom goosed the car backward and pulled a tight U-turn. Driving as fast as the potholed road allowed, it took almost twenty-five minutes to reach Highway 89.

On the way, Suzanne kept checking for cellphone service. "It's dead," she complained, doing her best to remain calm.

"Keep trying," Tom urged as the Chevy jolted up and down. "There's service all along the highway, and we're not that far away."

Eight minutes later, Suzanne's phone lit up. She punched Derek's number and quickly filled him in.

"Where are you?" he asked.

"We're on a mining track heading to 89, about fourteen miles north of the city limits."

"Okay. Stop when you hit the highway. I'll have a deputy out there within minutes. We'll try to nab the shooter. You're both okay?"

Soon, they spotted Deputy Angela Harper leaning against her patrol car, right at the turnoff. She waved to them as Tom brought the Chevy to a halt. The twins jumped out.

"The sheriff ordered a roadblock on 89 outside the city limits," the deputy informed them. "And we've got a couple of officers searching old mining roads farther north." Just then, a low-flying helicopter swooped past them overhead, heading westward. "That'll be Sheriff McClennan."

Everyone watched as the chopper traced parallel lines above the meadowlands. There wasn't a rider anywhere. At one stage, the pilot and the sheriff spotted the remains of the drone. They landed to pick up the pieces, but the only visible evidence was a neat hole through its underbelly and a much larger jagged-edged exit wound on top.

A siren began wailing in the distance. Two minutes later, Derek pulled up in his unmarked police car, Pete and Kathy in tow.

Kathy rushed over to the twins. "You both okay?"

"We're fine," Suzanne replied, nodding. "The shooter never saw us, we're pretty sure, but he sure brought down the drone."

"It happened so fast, you couldn't believe it," Tom said, pulling out his cellphone. "Check it out. Suzanne had the bird about four hundred feet up, heading back toward us."

Everyone gathered around as Tom hit Play on his phone. One second the drone's camera was capturing a spectacular view of the meadowlands. Then five shots rang out, loud enough to overcome the sound of the hammering wind. As the drone tumbled from the sky, Tom's screen displayed dizzying shards alternating between sky and earth. Then, silence.

"Gotta be an excellent shot to take down that bird," Pete declared.

Deputy Harper chuckled. "I dunno. A hundred plus yards is not far for a decent marksman . . . even with a moving target. The shooter took five shots, and only one of them hit the drone. Just plain lucky, I'd say."

"That's a fact," Derek agreed.

"We'll have to tell Ray about the drone," Suzanne said. "That's a call I don't look forward to."

"I'll call Ray," Tom volunteered. "As a member of the tech

club, I'm responsible for the borrowed equipment. I guaranteed its safety."

Deputy Harper shielded her eyes. "Looks like the sheriff is coming in for a visit."

13

A TRAP

The helicopter landed a hundred yards west of the highway. Soon, a small group had gathered beside the patrol car.

"We need to catch this person," Derek said, "and quickly too."

The sheriff agreed. "You're not kidding. First Wakefield's shot, then he's attacked in Intensive Care, now your drone is taken out. With the same rifle, I'd bet." He paused for a few seconds. "You know why, right?"

"Yup, competition," Pete said.

"Correct. The shooter's worried someone else will get to Rattler Mine first."

Suzanne brought up something that had troubled the two girls. "Remember the scene at the hospital?"

"What, specifically?" the sheriff asked.

"When the techs found the tissue with lipstick on it," Kathy replied. "In the tree."

"Sure. What about it?"

"Way too convenient," Suzanne said. "I mean, what are the odds?"

Deputy Harper nodded. "You know, when I first heard the story, it made me wonder. A tissue doesn't just 'fall out' of a woman's pocket."

"Plus, who would wipe off their lipstick to climb a tree?" Kathy said.

"Point taken," Derek said.

"Another thing," Kathy added. "The hospital attack on Mr. Wakefield was also weird. Turning his monitors and the other equipment off triggered alarms. The perp *had* to know that would happen."

Pete's head snapped up. "*Of course.* That explains why he stood by the door, waiting for the first person to rush in. He expected a nurse, not Suzanne, but it didn't matter. The perp couldn't have cared less. He had a *plan.*"

Tom nodded in agreement. "It makes perfect sense! The whole exercise was nothing but a false flag. A deliberate attempt to lead authorities away from the man who shot Mr. Wakefield! It was a *man* with a wig, not a woman with long grey hair. The point was to misdirect the Sheriff's Office into a search for an unknown female."

The sheriff chuckled. "So it's a guy, not a gal. And a smart one too. You might be on to something. He played us."

"He won't play us any longer," Derek said forcefully. "Right now, he's panicked about someone else finding the mine. It's gotta be close by, or he thinks it is. He doesn't want anyone poking around."

"Tom and Pete found prints from that distinctive horse-shoe with the bent nail yesterday," Suzanne said grimly.

"At the oasis," Pete added.

"The guy's tenacious," the sheriff said. "Give him that."

"Anything interesting on the roadblock?" Deputy Harper asked.

"Nothing," Derek replied. "The deputies stopped two horse trailers. They checked the horseshoes, but no match."

"It's possible the shooter's still around here," the deputy said.

"Anything's possible," the sheriff said. "But we never spotted a rider. With all these old mining claims, he and his horse could hide in any number of tunnels—then reappear at night. That'd be my best guess."

Derek's eyes ticked over to the twins. "I wonder why he didn't come after you?"

"We parked in a gully, right where the road ends," Suzanne explained. "No way would the shooter have seen us."

"Okay. That makes sense."

"I don't see the perp giving up his hunt," Pete said. "He's nearing the end game."

"I agree with Derek," Suzanne said. "We need to nab him before someone else gets hurt."

The officers chuckled.

"Great idea," the sheriff said. "How should we go about that?"

"Put teams out here," Suzanne suggested. "Hide them in the oasis with binoculars and two-way radios. No horses."

Kathy groaned. Stakeouts—and snakes. *What could be worse?*

The sheriff nodded. "I like it. Too bad I don't have the human resources."

Pete jumped at the idea. "The four of us can handle it in two teams. We can drive to the end of this track and hike in. Three miles at the most takes us to the oasis."

Tom raised an arm. "Count me in."

"Great!" Derek said. "The Sheriff's Office will provide two-way radios. They're powerful five-watt units, capable of reaching headquarters, even out here in the meadowlands."

The sheriff smiled. "Okay. I love your enthusiasm, but no hero stuff. You see a rider, you call for help. Right?"

THAT EVENING, THE FOUR MET AT THE JACKSONS' HOUSE. Sherri didn't appreciate their new plan. Not at all.

"Why are you putting yourself in so much danger? I don't like this."

The Chief argued in favor of the mystery searchers. "Sherri, there's nothing to worry about. They've got powerful two-way radios that connect to the Sheriff's Office. You can spot a horse and rider a mile away. They'll have plenty of warning."

"Easy to hide in the oasis too," Tom said. "It's encircled by huge weeping willows as wide as they are tall. No one would have a clue we're out there."

"You'll never convince me."

"Oh, Mom . . ." the twins chorused.

"How many times have I heard that?" But she gave in, later . . . grudgingly.

The foursome flipped coins to pick teams. Pete and Suzanne won and selected the first watch, beginning at six the next morning.

"That's the dream shift," Kathy groused. "It'll still be nice and cool. But by noon—when Tom and I show—it'll be stinking hot out there."

"Oh, well," Pete bugged.

She shot him one of her famous looks.

"It's the same stuff we need on every stakeout," Suzanne said, starting a list titled *Stuff to take.* "Water, snacks, flashlights, sandwiches, books . . ."

Derek had dropped off the two-way radios earlier. "Oh, man," Pete said, clicking the Talk button. "These are so cool."

14

A DISCOVERY

Suzanne picked up Pete at 5:00 a.m. on Thursday. Kathy greeted her best friend at the front door.

"I had to drag the big guy out of bed," she said, grinning. "If he falls asleep on you, give him a good kick." Fits of laughter rang out.

"Yeah, yeah," Pete muttered, pushing between them. Getting up early wasn't his thing. "I've heard this tune before. Let's roll."

The thirty-minute drive north on Highway 89 zipped by with almost no traffic. Suzanne spotted the old miner's road and hung a sharp left. "Okay," she warned. "This is where it gets rough. Hang tight."

Only a day earlier, she had driven the identical track with Tom, negotiating the giant potholes. The previous experience helped. Another twenty minutes passed before she pulled the Chevy into the same gorge as before. "End of the line."

"This is it?" Pete asked.

"Yup. From here on, we walk. Grab your backpack."

The two had dressed for a summer hike on the meadowlands: boots, shorts, light tops, hats, and sunglasses. They climbed out of the gorge and headed in a southwesterly direction. The oasis, they knew, couldn't be any farther than three miles. Soon enough, they spotted the weeping willows from a distance and adjusted their route into a straight-line hike to their target.

They followed the horse trail down to the waterhole. It was Suzanne's first visit to the oasis, and its natural beauty took her breath away. "Whoa, this is cool, isn't it?"

Pete pointed out a few dried, hardened imprints of the distinct horseshoe with one bent nailhead. "The individual we're looking for is riding this horse. The tracks are dried out now, but they were moist and muddy yesterday."

Suzanne fell to one knee. "They're just like the horseshoe print beside the ravine. Bet anything we get a return visit."

They scouted out hiding places in the weeping willows. Sitting in a tall tree high above the ridge line offered excellent views, with no blind spots. Plus, the abundant foliage sheltered them. But hiding among the willow branches soon became rather uncomfortable. The two agreed to take turns.

"Half an hour is plenty," Suzanne said. "After that, you have to stretch your legs."

"Agreed," Pete said. "I'll hike around the ridge line for an all-around view. We'll switch every thirty minutes."

"Done."

Alone in the desolate northern meadowlands, Pete saw evidence of wildlife: in the distance, a herd of elk cantered across the landscape; birds wheeled and shrieked, including a hawk that banked in the sky, swooping down for lunch. Pete watched, transfixed, as a nimble rabbit escaped. The hawk circled up again, only to continue the dance.

The two sleuths had switched places several times when,

a little after eleven o'clock, Suzanne scouted around the small, scenic pond, wondering about the underground water source. She found that she could walk three-quarters of the pond's circumference in less than a minute; access to the remaining quarter appeared to be blocked by a sheer rocky outcropping that had to be fifteen feet high. *Like a pyramid of rocks,* she thought. But at its base there appeared a two-foot-wide platform of solid earth bordering the water. Suzanne edged her way along it. "Hey, Pete!"

"Hey, yourself."

"There's blood down here."

"Blood?"

"Yup."

Pete scurried down from the willow tree where he was sitting and dropped to the ground. "What are you talking about?"

"Look for yourself."

Pete edged along the earthen platform. Suzanne, standing sideways to the rocky outcropping, pointed to three large splashes of dried blood on the rock wall.

"See?" Suzanne asked.

Pete went quiet for a few seconds. "Do I ever. Wait a sec. Do you think this is where Mr. Wakefield got it?"

"Well, someone did, that's for sure."

"Unless it's animal blood," Pete said.

"Yeah. Maybe."

"It couldn't be Wakefield," Pete argued. "I mean, what would he be doing here, standing on this—this little patch of earth." His eyes widened. *"Rattler Mine."*

"My thought exactly," Suzanne said.

Both dropped to their knees and hung their heads over the edge of the narrow earthen platform. Then they straightened up and locked eyes.

Pete dropped his voice down to a stage whisper. *"There's a space down there."*

They had both seen it: a tunnel, with its upper edge inches above the water—an aperture that appeared to extend three or four feet below the waterline.

"I'm going in," Suzanne declared.

Pete yanked off his boots and socks, then his T-shirt, and leaped into the pool. "I'll take a quick look."

"You need a flashlight!" Suzanne shouted.

Too late. Pete had already slipped below the earthen platform. He kicked his feet and disappeared through the tunnel's opening.

Suzanne raced off and dragged her backpack out from behind a tree. She dug out her waterproof flashlight just as Pete's head broke the surface. She ran back down to the water's edge.

"Suzanne!" he gasped, breathing hard, "there's a cavern down there with a stream running through it. We need a flashlight!"

"Here," she said dryly, handing it over.

"Oh, thanks. What about the two-way radio?"

"What about it? They're not waterproof."

"Right."

Suzanne pulled off her boots and socks and jumped into the pond. She slipped under the surface, following Pete as he crossed beneath the earthen platform where they had been standing. They surfaced and swam straight ahead until they found solid ground rising beneath their feet.

Suzanne gasped in astonishment when Pete clicked her flashlight on. They had entered a natural underground cavern hidden behind the rocky outcrop at the pond's edge— dark and dank, but beautiful in its own way—that had to be twenty feet high and just as wide. A narrow stream split the cavern into two, its bubbly sound bouncing off the high walls. The strong, pungent smell of decaying plant material filled their nostrils.

Behind them, sunlight reflected off the surface of the pond and shimmered off the walls and ceiling, which were otherwise lit only by the flashlight.

The two crept along one side of the stream.

"This place makes my skin crawl," Suzanne muttered.

"Are you putting me on?" Pete said. "We just found Rattler Mine!"

"We don't know that. Not yet anyway. We just found— something . . ." Seconds passed. "Pete, what is that?"

"What's what?"

"Up there, on the wall. I heard— It's moving! What the—"

Pete shot his beam of light up the wall. "Bats," he said nonchalantly and kept walking.

"Bats?"

"Uh-huh. Dozens of them. Don't let 'em bother you. They're nocturnal."

"Lovely."

Pete picked up a small piece of shiny rock and scrutinized it. "Think this is gold?"

Suzanne shrugged. "I dunno."

They walked for about twenty-five yards before the ceiling began sloping downward and the walls closed in, right where the stream entered the cavern from somewhere beneath the cave floor.

"The end," Pete said.

"We'd better get back there. Tom and Kathy should be close."

At that moment, an odd rumbling sound occurred. It lasted three or four seconds and repeated twice more before the rumble became a roar. The ground shuddered beneath their feet. Ten seconds later, the noise and the trembling stopped. The bats stirred, more restlessly.

"What was that?" Pete asked, wide-eyed and frozen in his tracks.

Without realizing it, Suzanne had grabbed his arm. "Was it—it felt like an earthquake!"

They rushed back to the water's edge. Suzanne's heartbeat ratcheted up as she glanced into the water. "Pete!"

"What?"

"There's no light coming from the entrance!"

"That's not even possible."

"Are we in the right place?"

Pete illuminated the cave floor, still wet from where they had crawled out of the water. "Uh-huh."

"Oh, boy," Suzanne whispered, almost to herself. "Not good."

"The water . . ." Pete said, sounding perplexed. "It's—it's like dirty brown. *What the—"*

Suzanne jumped in and submerged to search for the aperture. It wasn't possible to see a thing. The water was way too murky, and the sunlight outside seemed to have vanished. She reached out and touched something. Her hands searched . . . What? *Wait!* Rocks?

Uh-oh.

15

"WE'RE TOAST."

Tom stared at the pond in disbelief and shook his head. The day wasn't going well. Not at all.

First, there was the man on horseback. As they hiked in, they had spotted him in the distance, riding hard *away*, his horse kicking up a trail of dust behind him. Whoever he was, he had already traveled a mile or two north of the ravine.

"Pete and Suzanne *must* have seen him," Kathy declared. "By now the Sheriff's Office has deputies covering Highway 89."

"Yeah, it's possible," Tom said. He sounded doubtful.

Then they hiked into the oasis, arriving before noon, shocked to find no trace of Pete and Suzanne. Tom spotted his sister's backpack leaning against a tree. "Hey, that's Suzie's." He unzipped it to find her flashlight missing, and— he breathed a sigh of relief—the two-way radio buried at the bottom.

"Okay, you two," Kathy shouted out loud. "This isn't funny. Where ya' hiding? Come on out." No reply.

Tom stared at the water, worried and puzzled. It had a

muddy brown tinge that hadn't been there yesterday. *Wasn't like that last time . . . was it?* Then he remembered. He reached into his backpack, his hands searching for his cellphone. He dug it out and touched the camera icon.

Yesterday's final picture displayed a wide-angle view of the pond. The water was a bluish-green color. Not muddy brown. Worse, on the side opposite of where Tom and Kathy stood, above a rocky outcropping that plunged into the water, the rocks appeared in a pyramid formation that reached higher than it did now. *Much higher.* Now, the upper portion of the sloping hill was nothing but sandy-colored dirt.

"Kathy, they're behind those rocks!"

Alarm seeped into her voice. "What do you mean?"

"Look at this pic." He held the camera up to her face. "See the rock wall? It's partially collapsed, right into the pond. I'll bet anything that rider triggered a rockslide somehow. Pete and Suzie must've spotted something in there. That's why her flashlight is missing."

"Oh, Lord."

Tom pushed the Talk button on the two-way radio.

SUZANNE SURFACED AND SWAM OVER TO PETE. HE EXTENDED A hand and helped her clamber out of the water.

"We're trapped," she said. "Rocks have blocked the entrance to the cavern."

Pete groaned. "Oh, geez. We're toast."

"That's reassuring."

"Well, it's not like I'm trying to be negative," Pete said, sounding defensive.

"Really?" She coughed. "You could have fooled me."

"We can't assume the worst," Pete said, having just done

that. "We've got drinking water. It's a little chilly in here, but not bad. And about now, Tom and Kathy are searching for us. They'll find our backpacks and call for help. See?"

"I see. But those rocks didn't fall by themselves. Whoever shot down the drone must have caused the rockslide. You know why?"

"To ensure our destruction, for one thing."

"Uh-huh. But in the meantime, the bad guy blocked access to the cavern. You know what *that* means?"

"Uh . . . no, actually."

"It means this *isn't* Rattler Mine, silly! And he's already figured that out."

"Ah, yes," Pete picked up on her line of thinking. "But how would he even know we're in here?"

"My backpack."

"What about it?"

"I left it sitting by the pond."

Long pause. *"Hmm."* One thing about Pete—nothing much bothered him. "Oh. well. We're stuck now. Let's do a little exploring. Maybe there's another way outta here."

"Okay. But we gotta conserve the juice in this flashlight. It's not as if we have extra batteries."

"Good point. We'll do a once around, then shut it down."

They searched for a crevice, a tributary, a breath of fresh air—anything that offered a ray of hope. No such luck. Just dark, dampish walls that felt slimy and smelled worse.

At the far end, they beamed the flashlight into the running stream. Pete jumped in and submerged, searching for the water's source. The stream originated from an underground tunnel, as they had thought, but it was *way* too tight to negotiate.

He surfaced and rejoined Suzanne on firm ground, shivering for the first time. "No chance down there. We're stuck and I'm hungry."

"Better get used to it."

UP TOP, THINGS HAD SHIFTED INTO HIGH GEAR. NOT LONG After Kathy alerted the Sheriff's Office dispatcher, she and Tom spotted the Yavapai County Search and Rescue helicopter heading their way. It landed nearby, just twenty-one minutes after the emergency call. Four paramedics raced into the oasis.

Frank and Gary, the wranglers from the Flying W, arrived half an hour later, leading Derek and Sheriff McClennan on horseback. The Chief and Joe Brunelli were right behind them.

"Anything?" Joe asked, his face shrouded by concern.

"Nothing yet," Tom replied.

"They can handle it," the Chief assured Joe. The two friends had attended high school with Rob. Paramedics were already at work, shifting rocks and trying to prevent a further collapse.

People gathered around, talking in low tones as Tom and Kathy explained what had happened, and why they believed that something—*or someone*—had trapped Pete and Suzanne behind the rock wall. Kathy mentioned the rider they had seen on the way in.

Sheriff McClennan zoned in. "What time was this?"

"A quarter to twelve."

The sheriff cornered the two wranglers. "Can you pick up his trail?"

"It's difficult to track on this terrain," Gary replied, "especially on dry ground, but we'll sure try."

"Where's Rob?" the sheriff asked.

"Picking up supplies," Gary answered.

The first order of business, the removal of the collapsed rock wall, continued. The rescuers extracted single boulders, many of them weighing forty to fifty pounds each. For safety reasons, the paramedics attacked the project without help, as the experienced team they were. Everyone watched as one rock after another splashed into the center of the pond.

An hour passed before the wranglers returned. "No luck. He headed north, but we lost him before the highway," Frank reported.

After a lot of hard work, the paramedics reached the waterline. They displaced a final row of stones before one of them came up for air. "There's a tunnel under here!" she shouted.

SUZANNE SAT ON THE CAVERN FLOOR, WATCHING THE BLOCKED opening with bated breath. The thought of sitting in total darkness panicked her, so she kept insisting that Pete flick the light on, if only briefly. She kept one eye on the restless bats, and the other on the dark pond.

Pete paced back and forth like a caged animal.

Earlier, they heard a weird scratching sound. It carried on for quite some time before a loud *thud* reverberated off the cavern walls.

Pete whooped. "What'd I tell you? Help is on the way. Nothing to worry about."

"You didn't say that at all."

"Close enough."

Later, they watched in awe as a thin ray of light filtered through the aperture and into the murky water. More scrapings and thuds occurred before it brightened by infinitesimal degrees.

Then a watery shadow appeared. Suzanne and Pete leaped to their feet as a woman in a wetsuit surfaced inside the cavern, right in front of them.

"You both okay?" she asked.

"Overjoyed!" Pete shouted.

"Are we ever!" Suzanne cried out, jumping into the water.

16

A RETURN VISIT

E vening came. An impromptu party had erupted at the Brunellis' house.

Maria served one of her finest Italian dinners: a caprese salad with pesto sauce and linguini con pomodoro e basilico. Her tomato-basil sauce was famous. She followed up with her delicious homemade spumoni ice cream cake.

"*Mmm-mmm*, the best," Suzanne said as she finished up a bowlful. The Chief and Sherri agreed. They had never tasted better. The twin's father surprised them when he accepted a second helping. The Chief had always labored to stay in shape and seldom touched deserts.

"This is why I count calories," Kathy whispered to her best friend between bites.

That night, laughter flowed nonstop at the Brunelli household. The rescue at the oasis had invigorated everyone —dinner was a celebration filled with gratefulness. Later, before the Jackson family headed home, the conversation rotated back to the legend of Rattler Mine.

"We need to confirm Suzanne's suspicion," Tom declared, "that the cavern in the oasis is *not* Rattler Mine."

Pete was still busy stuffing his face. "Not a shred of doubt in my mind."

"Meaning what?" his sister challenged.

"Meaning someone spilled Mr. Wakefield's blood out there for a reason. We can't rule out anything yet."

Suzanne rolled her eyes. "If the perp knew the cavern was Rattler Mine, there's no way he'd block the entrance. *He* had already ruled it out. Where's that piece of ore you found?"

"Oh, yeah. I forgot all about it." He reached into his jeans pocket and retrieved a small sample of ore, a rough cube, half an inch on each side. As it traveled around the table, comments flew back and forth.

"I don't see any gold," Joe said, examining every side.

"Might contain some silver," the Chief figured. He bounced it in the palm of his hand. "Gold and silver are often mined together. It's sure heavy enough for its size."

"How can you tell for sure?" Maria asked.

"You can't, not really," Kathy replied. "But there's an assayer downtown who's good at this stuff."

"Let's run it past him," Tom said. "Meanwhile, we'll rent a metal detector from Hall's Hardware and check out the cavern."

"Wait a second," Sherri said, sitting straight up in alarm. "You're not going out there again?"

"It's okay, Mom," Suzanne said. "Derek Robinson is coming with us."

"I don't like it."

"Me neither," Maria agreed. "It's dangerous out there."

"What do you think?" Joe asked, looking toward the Chief.

"Derek Robinson is an experienced detective," he replied

firmly. "He'll be armed and on the lookout for anything suspicious. I don't foresee a problem."

ON FRIDAY MORNING, AT 9:00 A.M., THE MYSTERY SEARCHERS gathered behind Hall's Hardware and walked through the back door.

"Hi, Mr. Hall!" Tom called out.

"Hey, it's the twins," the storekeeper replied, stepping over with an outstretched hand. "And Pete and Kathy. Welcome!" Mr. Hall's reputation as the friendliest guy in Prescott was well deserved. Tom often thought he should run for mayor. "How are the mystery searchers doing?"

The girls smiled and shook hands with him. "We're great, Mr. Hall," Kathy replied.

Pete asked, "Can we rent a metal detector—one that can locate gold?"

"Follow me."

Minutes later, the foursome jumped into the Chevy. Suzanne drove straight out on Highway 89 to rendezvous with Derek Robinson. He had left earlier and parked his unmarked cruiser at the mining road turnoff. Both cars continued along the track before halting in the gorge. The five of them began their hike in the ever-increasing desert heat. Three miles later, the group descended the sloping path to the pond, grateful for the cooling water.

"Who's going under?" Derek asked, pointing to the aperture at the water' edge.

Pete was already pulling off his shirt and shorts to reveal bathing trunks. Both Suzanne and Pete had been pretty darn uncomfortable heading home in their soaking wet clothes the day before. This time, all four mystery searchers had come prepared to swim.

"Wouldn't miss it for the world," Pete said before leaping into the pond.

Tom carried the gold metal detector, sealed in a black plastic garbage bag to protect it from the water, and another flashlight. "Me too." He tore off his outer clothing and disappeared beneath the surface.

Kathy glanced over at Suzanne for reassurance. "No snakes in there, right?"

"Nope, we didn't spot one."

"Okay." The girls splashed in, also armed with waterproof flashlights.

Derek trekked back up the trail and circled the oasis. In one hand, he carried a set of binoculars; in the other, a two-way radio.

Kathy surfaced inside the cavern, awed by her first look at the underground wonder. "*Wow!* Talk about jaw-dropping."

Pete had already crawled out of the water and clicked on his flashlight. He reached out to his sister and helped pull her to dry land. "Told ya. Isn't this something?"

Tom passed the metal detector up to the Brunellis. "It sure is!" He grabbed Suzanne's hand and helped her scramble up. Soon, three other flashlights lit up, shooting beams of light the length and breadth of the cavern's interior.

"Ugh, the walls are slimy," Kathy complained.

"They smell bad too," Suzanne said. "Rotting vegetation filtering down from the surface somehow. See all the plant roots?" She aimed her flashlight at the ceiling.

Pete scoffed. "What'd you expect, wallpaper? Except for Wakefield, I'd bet we're the only people who've ever been in here."

"*If* that was his blood," Kathy said.

"Who else's?"

"Who knows?"

Suzanne pointed high up the walls. "Kathy, check out the bats,"

"Bats don't scare me. They only travel at night."

Tom stripped away the garbage bag and flipped on the metal detector's switch.

"How does that thing work, anyway?" Kathy asked.

"It transmits an electromagnetic field into the ground," Tom explained. "Then it analyzes the return, which is known as an eddy current and has its *own* electromagnetic field. By measuring the size of the eddy currents and how fast they're traveling, a gold detector calculates the 'time constant' of a target. Gold has a longer time constant than, say, bits of aluminum. And when it detects gold, it beeps like crazy. The higher the pitch, the more metal. Get it?"

Kathy blinked. "I think so."

For the next hour, the foursome explored the cavern, scanning the ground and reaching as high up the walls as possible. The detector found minute traces of gold, causing the machine to beep. Occasionally, the sound rose to a higher frequency for a second or two but then quickly fell silent.

"Dead end," Suzanne said later. "There's not even one whole ounce of gold here total. It sure isn't Rattler Mine."

"How strange," Kathy said, a puzzled look crossing her face. "What the heck was Mr. Wakefield doing in here?"

17

RATTLER MINE

Saturday, right after breakfast, Kathy's cellphone buzzed. "Hi, Mom."

Maria worked the dayshift in the Emergency Unit at Prescott Regional Hospital. "You'll never guess what. Mr. Wakefield is conscious!"

"You gotta be kidding," Kathy put the call on speaker.

"Nope. A nurse in Intensive Care told me. He woke up about an hour ago but couldn't talk. The hospital called Cynthia Myers—she had herself listed as next of kin—and she's on her way. They also alerted Detective Robinson a short time ago."

At that second, Suzanne's cellphone buzzed.

"Hi, Derek."

"Wakefield came out of his coma. I'm heading over."

"Us too."

"See you there." *Click.*

Ten minutes later, the foursome trod quietly into Herb Wakefield's hospital room. Things had changed since their last visit. Most of the medical technology and tubes had disappeared, so there were noticeably fewer electronic bleeps and blips.

Cynthia Myers sat in a chair on the far side, holding Herb's hand. Opposite her stood Derek Robinson. He glanced over his shoulder as the foursome trooped in.

"Herb," Cynthia said, "these are the four young people who saved your life."

Mr. Wakefield tilted his head, taking in their faces one by one. Seconds passed by before a tiny smile crossed his face. "Thank you," he said in a raspy voice.

Derek repeated a question. "Again, who shot you, sir?"

The older man's eyes lifted toward the detective. "I, uh . . . swam out of the tunnel, climbed out of the water . . . heard a shot . . . remember little else."

"Why were you there?" Suzanne asked.

"Exploring."

"Who wanted you dead?" Derek pushed.

"Don't know . . ."

Tom leaned forward. "Mr. Wakefield, who else knew about Rattler Mine?"

Bleary eyes shot over to Tom in surprise. "No one . . . Cynthia"—he turned toward her—"was the only one . . . trusted."

Derek's head swiveled toward her.

"Herb," she protested, "I don't have a clue where your mine is."

"Mailed you . . . directions," he said.

"When?"

"Day before." His eyes closed as he drifted off.

"Oh, my gosh," Cynthia said, wiping away tears. "I pick my mail up on Mondays. I guess there'll be a letter waiting for me."

"We'll need to see that, Cynthia," Derek said.

"What for?" she said. A suspicious look crossed her face.

"Evidence. The shooter might have found the mine. We have to check out everything. Why are you acting defensively?"

"I'm trying to protect Herb, that's why."

"Well, you're not helping him. The contents of that letter are critical, and there might be fingerprints on it."

Seconds passed in silence before Cynthia sighed. "Okay. I guess I understand. I'll drive over to the Wickenburg post office on my way home. It'll be in my box there. I'll call you."

The mystery searchers waited in anticipation. Pete paced the Jackson's living room. Finally, right after lunch, Tom's cellphone buzzed.

"Okay, we got it," Derek Robinson began. "Herb provided Cynthia with the exact coordinates of the mine, latitude and longitude. So we'll need to determine that in the meadowlands."

Tom put the call on speaker. "No problem at all. I've got an app for that on my cell."

"Cellphones don't work out there."

As a core member of Prescott High's technology club, Tom had certain advantages. "It's true that cell service is very patchy out in the meadowlands. But the GPS can still work even if the phone can't make or receive calls and has no access to data," he explained. "Smartphones are receivers. Just the way your radio receives a signal from a radio station, GPS-enabled devices like a smartphone act like an antenna that receives a signal from a GPS satellite network. A computer chip allows the cell to process the Assisted GPS signal and calculate a location. Simple, right?"

"If you say so," Derek replied, chuckling. "Okay. Let's take a spin out there. No horses, either. We'll walk in so that we're not so visible. When can you all be ready?"

Suzanne placed a call to Heidi Hoover and filled her in. "We're heading out there with Derek in an hour. Want to join in the fun?"

"I sure do," Heidi said, "but I'm working on a breaking story. Can you send me directions? I'll drive out as soon as possible."

"You bet," Suzanne replied. "I'll text you a map with the exact turnoff. Hang a left until you see our parked cars. Then follow the trail. But it's a three-mile hike—bring water."

"Got it."

As the afternoon temperature exploded upward, Derek and the foursome arrived at the exact latitude and longitude provided by Cynthia, smack in the middle of the meadowlands. Just as he had promised, Tom's phone's geolocation app worked. He checked the numbers for the umpteenth time: 34.690482, −112.472087. A quarter mile away, the tops of the weeping willows swayed in the breeze.

"Someone's putting us on," Pete groused. "There's nothing here but grass."

"Unless Herb or Cynthia erred," Kathy suggested.

Derek pulled his hat lower. His freckled face always took a beating from the scorching sun. "I had Cynthia read the numbers three times. Any error wouldn't be on her. Unless—"

"She did it on purpose," Pete said, finishing his thought.

"No way," Suzanne dismissed the idea.

Tom ambled in tight concentric circles, eyeing his cellphone screen at the same time. "Be quiet, you guys. I hear something."

"Such as?" Pete asked,

"Well, I— It's so faint, but . . . running water."

Everyone stopped in their tracks. "It's the wind," Pete argued.

"Hush." Suzanne walked up beside her brother. "You're right, Tom. I hear it as well."

Kathy's eyes widened. "Me too."

"Here," Tom murmured. "Look under this huge rock."

They all fell to their knees and bent down. High grass enveloped a flat stone slab, five feet across, almost concealing it from view. Underneath one side was a space just over a foot high. Pete pulled a flashlight from his backpack and shot a beam into the darkness. The space appeared to expand, first outward, then downward. Pete pushed himself farther in. The faint sound of moving water grew louder.

"*Game on!*" Pete yelled. "Follow me."

Suzanne startled him. "I'm right behind you."

"You guys go ahead," Derek called out. "I need to keep an eye open up top. Shout if you find anything interesting."

Pete beamed his cellphone flashlight into the darkness beneath the slab and spotted firm ground below, about five feet down. The space immediately below appeared to merge into a wider tunnel. Pete wriggled forward on his belly and then, swinging his legs ahead, he dropped, landing on both feet beside a four-foot-wide shallow stream.

"I'm in!" he shouted, looking up and behind him. "Nothing to it!"

Suzanne landed right next to him. "Tom, you coming?"

They watched Tom's legs swing outward before he pushed himself off the ledge. "Where's Kathy?"

"I'm here. Watch out!"

Flashlights clicked on. "Ladies and gentlemen, welcome to Rattler Mine," Pete murmured.

The similarities between the cavern in the oasis and Rattler Mine startled them—a rushing stream with a wet earthen pathway on either side, slimy walls, scattered rocks of every shape and size—and an awful, acrid mildewy smell that assaulted their nostrils. And bats hanging on the ceiling.

No wonder it smells in here, Suzanne thought.

But the cave's ceiling appeared much lower than the oasis cavern's and, from where they stood, the tunnel ahead seemed endless. They followed along one side of the stream, their phone flashlight beams pointing the way forward.

Every so often, one or the other picked up a rock. "Gold, for sure," Pete said, convinced he held a fortune in his hand.

Kathy giggled.

That's when they caught sight of something else, a few yards in front. Something white and long. And blocking their path.

"What is it?" Pete asked.

Tom drew closer, cautiously. "It's a skeleton."

"A skeleton . . ." the others chorused.

"Uh-huh. The human kind."

"Creep me out, why don't you?" Suzanne whispered to no one specifically.

The mystery searchers bent over and examined the bones under the glare of their flashlights. "This guy won't hurt us," Tom said. "He's been dead a century or more, I'd guess."

"The missing prospector," Pete surmised. He checked the expression on Kathy's face. "So maybe it's true," he needled. "Maybe a rattlesnake got the guy."

Kathy pulled an immediate U-turn. "That's it for me."

18

THE MYSTERY MAN

As Kathy clamored out from under the slab, Derek's two-way radio beeped twice. A metallic voice radioed, "Headquarters to Detective Robinson."

He touched the Talk button. "This is Derek."

"I have an urgent message for you from Heidi Hoover from *The Daily Pilot*."

"Go ahead."

"It reads, 'Company coming your way. A truck and horse trailer turned into the meadowlands from Highway 89 and headed east. I'm fourteen miles north of the city limits.' End of message."

"Thank you. Can you transfer me to Sheriff McClennan?"

"Yes, sir. Hold on."

Kathy dug her binoculars out of her backpack and trained them eastward, scanning north to south. "Yup, there he is. A mile away and heading our way . . . from the far side of the oasis." *Can't be a coincidence . . .*

Derek spotted him too. "Any idea who he is?"

"Nope, not at this distance," she replied.

The detective poked his head under the slab and yelled. "Come on out, guys! We've got a visitor we have to deal with! Let's go tunneling later."

Soon, the threesome scrambled up the tunnel, helping one another out of the hidden entrance.

"Keep down," Derek ordered. "He doesn't have a clue we're out here—not yet anyway."

The five flattened themselves, bellies down on the warm earth.

The two-way radio beeped twice. "McClennan here."

"Sheriff, it's Derek Robinson. I'm out on the meadowlands with the mystery searchers. We have a horseback rider heading our way, about a mile out. I'll try to intercept him, but I might need help."

"Any idea where his entry point is?"

"Heidi Hoover spotted him exiting Highway 89 about fourteen miles north of the city limits."

"Great. I'll get a deputy out your way. Meanwhile, we'll arrange a welcoming committee."

"Ten-four. I'll keep you informed on my end."

Derek passed his binoculars around. "He's still quite a ways out there. Anyone recognize him?"

One by one, the mystery searchers peered through the binoculars and shook their heads. "Nope."

"Me neither."

"Too far away," Suzanne said. "But it looks like a guy."

With no warning, the rider stopped short. One hand shielded his eyes as he stared their way. Then he pulled a fast U-turn, galloping back in the same direction he had come.

"W-what the heck?" Pete stammered.

"My fault, sorry," Derek replied. He jumped to his feet. "Let's go. I think the sun glinted off my binoculars and spooked him. He's worried about riding into a trap."

"That's funny," Suzanne said. "That's where he's heading right now."

Halfway back to their cars, they spotted Heidi Hoover trekking out in their direction.

As she got closer, Heidi shouted, "Did you guys get my message?"

"We sure did," the detective replied. "Thank you."

"You're welcome."

"The Sheriff's Office is looking for the guy," Kathy informed her.

"Did you get a license plate number on the trailer?" Tom asked.

"I did not. He was too far ahead."

"It was a male, right?" Pete asked.

"For sure."

"Follow us," Derek instructed. "I promised that you'd get your story. Let's see who they reeled in."

Soon, with Derek leading, the three vehicles headed back on the old miners' road toward 89. Once he reached the highway, the detective flipped on his emergency lights and hit the siren, racing southward. Two other cars trailed close behind.

As traffic pulled over to make way, Pete couldn't believe how much fun it was. "Hey, this is *great!*"

Five minutes later, three cruisers from the Sheriff's Office appeared on the west side of 89. They had blocked a truck and horse trailer from entering the highway. A knot of deputies stood next to the trailer, talking.

The three-car cavalcade pulled to a stop. The mystery searchers, Heidi, and Derek all jumped out of their vehicles and raced to the scene.

Deputy Angela Harper greeted them as they grew closer.

"Hey, over here," she shouted. Heidi's camera captured images on the run. *Click. Click. Click.*

"You know this guy?" Deputy Harper asked. "He refuses to talk to us." A smallish man sat on the ground, leaning against a cruiser, his arms handcuffed behind him. As they approached, he looked up.

The mystery searchers stopped in shock. Kathy exclaimed, "Walt McLaughlin!"

19

LUCKY STRIKE

Herbert W. Wakefield woke up to a new world. He found himself famous overnight.

After Heidi filed her story on Saturday night, news services from across the country picked it up. By Monday morning, the blockbuster report had hit the major networks. And why not? Mr. Wakefield had rediscovered Rattler Mine, a legendary gold mine lost for a century and a half. Perhaps the richest mine in Arizona history.

Cynthia, with the help of the Yavapai County Sheriff's Office, filed a mining claim in Mr. Wakefield's name that morning.

Meanwhile, at Prescott Regional Hospital, Dr. Truegood said he'd never seen anything like it. "I can't even get into the room," he complained. But against all odds, his patient had survived. The doctor wore a smile.

Downstairs, strangers who hadn't ever *met* the man vied for visitor passes. But Sheriff McClennan forbade all visitors. And he ordered the security service to bar reporters too.

Except Heidi Hoover, of course. She received special treatment.

Cynthia sat on one side of Herb's bed, overjoyed that her good friend had survived—and prospered. Meanwhile, Derek picked Rosemary up from Courthouse Square and escorted her to the second-floor room. For the first time, she learned about Rattler Mine.

"And here I figured you were just another prospector dreaming of hitting it big," she quipped.

"I'll be coming to see you," Mr. Wakefield said.

"I'll count on it," she replied before ducking out.

Heidi and Derek stood against one wall, right beside the Chief and a beaming Sheriff McClennan. The four mystery searchers squeezed in around the end of the bed.

The Sheriff's Office still had questions. Derek's bright red nose flared, burnt from the summer sun on the meadowlands. "Mr. Wakefield, it's my understanding you used to take samples of ore to McLaughlin. Why did you stop using his services?"

"Spent a quarter century of my life looking for Rattler Mine," he answered. "I made the mistake of telling Walt that I felt like I was getting closer." He caught his breath. Cynthia gave him a sip of water. "He started asking too many questions."

"When?"

"Two months ago, I'd guess."

Heidi asked, "How did you locate the mine?"

"The underground stream . . . I just followed it," Mr. Wakefield replied. "From the oasis. I made some guesses about its path. Even then, it was a lucky strike. What tipped me off was hearing running water under that big slab. If I hadn't heard it . . ."

Heads nodded around the hospital room. "Yup," Pete said. "We get it."

Tom had a question. "McLaughlin shot you after you exited the cavern. Why there?"

"My guess is he figured that's where the mine was. I had been there once before . . . shortly before I first discovered the stream." He chuckled. Seconds passed while he coughed. "He must have been following me, watching me, without my knowing. And he had to have been awful disappointed . . . shooting me for nothing. There's no gold to speak of in that cavern."

"He's an assayer," Suzanne noted. "He would have figured that out as soon as he got in there."

"That's a fact," Kathy said.

"So he'd been tracking you for some time . . ." Pete said.

"I guess. Should have listened to my intuition. Sometimes, out in the meadowland, I sensed that I wasn't alone. Not all the time, mind you. Just . . ."

"McLaughlin's a little guy," Sheriff McClennan noted. "How did he get you back on your horse?"

"I have no idea."

"I think he floated Mr. Wakefield on to Sugarcane," Derek answered, "in the oasis."

"Floated him?"

"Uh-huh. When the wrangler located Sugarcane, her saddle and saddlebags were damp. At the time, I wondered why."

"Oh, sure," Tom said, catching Mr. Wakefield's eye. "Your clothes were damp when we found you. McLaughlin must've led Sugarcane into the water, then floated your body onto her back."

"The ore samples," Suzanne recalled, "stolen from your house in Wickenburg. Was that because of their value, or ...?"

105

"Well," Pete said, "they *are* worth a lot of dough."

"True," Derek said. "But McLaughlin wouldn't want anyone wondering where they came from. That's the reason he had to make sure they disappeared."

"Unfortunately for him," Cynthia said, "he left one sample behind."

"Correct," Sheriff McClennan said. "And just like bread-crumbs, that ore led to McLaughlin's front door." He winked at the mystery searchers. "When you showed up, I'm positive you panicked him, even if he didn't show it."

"You're right, Sheriff," Kathy said. "He put on a good show."

"Mr. Wakefield," the Chief asked, "did Walt McLaughlin know that you had helped Rosemary? Did you mention her name to him?"

He paused. "Yes."

"Did you tell him she had grey hair?"

"I think so."

Tom nodded. "That explains why he broke into your room. He wasn't trying to harm you further. His goal was to plant a false flag—to send the Sheriff's Office on a wild goose chase searching for a woman with grey hair."

Derek nodded. "McLaughlin's a wiry little guy and pretty darn thin. No wonder he fooled that nurse. That wig was a great ruse."

"How did he trigger that rockslide?" the sheriff asked. "That had to be tricky."

Derek shrugged. "We're not sure. The paramedics guessed that all he had to do was pull out two or three rocks. That started an avalanche. But unless he talks . . ."

Kathy asked, "What'll happen to him now?"

"He's all lawyered up," the sheriff growled, "and refuses to talk. But his horse has the shoe with the bent nail, and we've tied the bullets to his .30/06 Winchester."

"We also served a search warrant on his business premises," Derek told everyone for the first time. "Technicians found a dozen samples of crystalline gold hidden in a drawer with a false bottom—and we know where they came from. Mr. Wakefield can identify them, of course. And here's something interesting. McLaughlin had a sign taped on his front door: 'On vacation. Back on August first.'"

"Oh, wow," Kathy exclaimed. "That explains a lot. No wonder we crossed paths with him so often. He wasn't at work."

"That's right," Derek said. "But his *next* vacation is likely to be in Florence State Prison—with free meals included. We have a list of charges against him, some calling for long sentences—including attempted murder. We don't expect to see Mr. McLaughlin on the streets again. Not for a long, long time."

"Sorry to interrupt," Cynthia said. "I think we need to let Herb rest. He's getting tired."

"Okay, everybody out," the sheriff said.

Heidi got in the last word. "Can I get a pic of you and Cynthia?" she asked the prospector.

"Sure."

Cynthia leaned over and slipped her arm around Herb. They gazed into the lens and smiled. *Click.*

LATER THAT NIGHT, DEREK INVITED THE MYSTERY SEARCHERS to join him on a conference call. Something about good news, he texted beforehand.

"Cynthia called me a few minutes ago," he informed the foursome. "She said Herb wants to replace your drone. He told her you should buy the best one possible—no matter how expensive it is."

Tom whooped out loud. "Wow, that's great! Wait'll we tell Ray. That gets us out of a big fix."

"How much can you spend on one of those things?" Kathy asked.

"A lot," Tom replied. "Thousands, even. We wouldn't do that, would we?"

"No," Suzanne said firmly. "We would not."

Pete grinned. *"Are you serious?* Of course we would!"

PREVIEW EXCERPT FROM BOOK 10

THE HAUNTING OF WAINRICH MANOR

1

The Target

"This place is downright spooky," Kathy said, her voice hushed.

Pete squinted in the dark, cold night. "Well, duh. Anytime there are ghosts running around . . ."

Kathy clucked like a hen. "You and your ghosts."

Pete grinned. He loved annoying his sister.

It was close to midnight. For the past hour, the lookalike siblings had scrunched down, sheltering behind a line of barren oak trees, their eyes locked on the forsaken One Wainrich Manor. Their hiding place afforded views of the front of the imposing three-story mansion, which faced east, and the side of the house, facing south. *Dark as the ace of spades.*

They had been in the same position for so long that

Kathy had developed leg cramps. *Not to mention being half frozen,* she brooded. Moonlight reflected off patches of white, the remnants of a recent after-Christmas snowfall in Prescott. A million stars winked down at them. Lying on the hard, cold ground—with nothing between them and the earth but a thin, old comforter—was a sure recipe for torture. Plus, she hated stakeouts with a passion. Above all, there was the boredom factor. Time crawled by in slow motion.

As the minutes clicked toward midnight, Pete began losing hope. Kathy checked her cellphone for the umpteenth time. "We're outta here in fifteen," she insisted. "Not another—"

"There it is!" Pete blurted. A flickering light had materialized on the manor's darkened third floor, glimmering through a dormer window. *Well, well.* The phenomenon had appeared just as Mrs. Robertson—Roberta, as she had insisted the siblings call her—had claimed it would. Next, she had said, it would work its way into the basement. *Why?* At this stage, there were no answers. Only questions.

Down, down went the quivering glow, reappearing in the windows of the second floor just moments later as it continued its journey through the mansion. Not that they could see its movement on the staircase—no windows there. The light vanished again. If it followed the path Roberta had first witnessed, then it would skip the ground floor and, well . . .

The mystery searchers had scouted the manor more than once. They knew the basement was windowless. Still, there was a multi-sided glass hatch on the south side of the home that topped what used to be a coal chute, a relic from the century before. Yellowed with age, filthy with grime, the multiple panes of glass hid whatever rested—or moved —beneath.

The siblings waited with bated breath, but not for long.

There. From inside the hatch, the glow filtered through the grimy glass. *Right where Roberta had said it would.* It seemed to float in the air forever. The two watched, transfixed, when—to their astonishment—the hatch opened upward with, seemingly, nothing beneath to push it open except the strange light. A few moments passed before the cover lowered and the quivering glow vanished. Darkness returned to One Wainrich Manor.

"Creepy!" Kathy whispered, grabbing her brother's arm without realizing it. Adrenalin coursed through her body. Her face was flushed, and she no longer felt frozen. Although Kathy emphatically did not believe in ghosts, she had a visceral reaction to uncanny phenomena.

Pete remained calm. "Did it—whatever *it* is—just escape from that open hatch?" he wondered aloud.

"There's no 'it,' there *can't* be an 'it,'" his sister chided. "Nothing escaped and whoever's still inside must be human."

"How do you know?"

"Please tell me you don't believe in ghosts."

"I . . . didn't—"

"Give me a break." Still, Kathy admitted to herself, what had occurred was—so far—unexplainable.

"Okay," Pete said. "Let's find out. We're going in there."

Kathy turned a critical eye toward her brother. "*We're* going in there.' Who is this 'we' you're referring to?"

"You and me, of course," Pete replied with a devilish grin. "If that glass hatch is unlocked, we've got an open invitation."

"I was afraid you'd say that."

"It's now or never."

"Personally, I think you're cra—"

Pete—ever the impulsive one of the pair who often moved too fast and talked too soon—didn't care. He leaped to his feet, raced out from behind the tree line, and scaled a hedge. He glanced back once, noting with satisfaction that Kathy was shadowing him. Their target, the yellowed glass hatch on the south side of the mansion, lay dead ahead.

What had replaced the old coal chute *under* the grimy glass relic they hadn't a clue. They had forgotten to ask Roberta about that, but it made no difference. The game plan was to gain access to the manor house, which had proved elusive. Until now. Maybe.

Pete reached the target, falling to his knees and breathing hard—not from fear, but from the frenzy of excitement. *Is this fun, or what?* He grasped hold of a rusty metal handle centered atop the hatch. "Here's hoping," he muttered.

Kathy stood behind him, clasping her hands together, whispering, "Not liking this. Just saying. There's someone in there."

Pete pulled on the handle. *Nothing.* He pulled harder. *Still nada.* He stood and, grabbing it again with both hands, fiercely determined, yanked hard, twisting his body more than halfway around in the effort. *Click!*

"Oh, Lord," Kathy muttered.

As Pete swung the hatch high enough to squeeze under, its hinges squealed with a mournful sound.

"Pete, you'll wake the dead," Kathy hissed.

"Stairs," he breathed. "Go down the stairs, Kathy."

"Me?" She glanced downward into near pitch darkness. Moonlight exposed the first two or three wooden steps, descending at a steep angle before fading into nothingness.

"Yes! Go. Now. This stupid hatch is freaking heavy. Don't worry. I'll be right behind you."

Kathy grasped her brother's shoulder for support and set

one foot on the first step. It was solid enough, which seemed oddly comforting. She paused, reaching for the cellphone in her back pocket.

"*No flashlight!*" Pete warned. "Not until we get down there."

"Who put you in charge?"

"Just do it! My arms are about to fall off."

"You're responsible if I break my neck."

"So noted."

She plunked herself down, sitting on the top step, bumping down one stair at a time, counting twelve before reaching hard, cold concrete under both feet. An awful smell greeted her—stale, moldy, and pervasive. "I'm on the basement floor," she called up, her voice hushed once again. "And it stinks to high heaven down here."

Something unseen scampered along the floor. Kathy wanted to scream as she drew her feet in closer. "There're *rats* down here!"

"You're surprised, after sixty years? I'm not."

"You're a regular genius."

Her brother, silhouetted against the moonlit night sky, twisted his body under the hatch and slipped down the top two stairs in a single step. Then he allowed the ancient relic to close behind him. Gently.

Click.

Kathy's ears perked up. "*Wait!* Did that thing just lock itself?"

Pete pushed up on the hatch, hard. "Well, it's stuck at least. I don't get it. It should open from the inside, but it won't move."

"Oh, Lord," his sister moaned again.

"Not a problem." He negotiated the stairs without a moment's hesitation, springing onto the concrete floor as if it were a basketball court. "Getting out of here will be easier than it was to get in."

"And you know this *how*?"

"That part is still unknown."

"Brilliant."

Kathy fired off a quick text message to the Jackson twins, Suzanne and Tom. Ever since graduating into Prescott High, the Jackson and Brunelli foursome had teamed up to solve mysteries and fight crime. *The Daily Pilot,* Prescott's hometown newspaper, and its star reporter, Heidi Hoover, had covered their cases, regularly plastering them across the front page. It was Heidi—who had soon become a best friend and often a fellow investigator too—who had dubbed the four young sleuths "the mystery searchers." The name had stuck.

Her hurried text read: *It's back! Made it into the mansion— thru the glass hatch.* She hit Send and muted her cell. Kathy knew that the keys to One Wainrich Manor would arrive the following day. *No more crazy stakeouts.* The thought filled her with a transitory moment of joy.

"It sure smells bad down here," Pete grumbled.

"I already told you that."

The siblings tapped the flashlight icons on their cellphones, projecting light that they filtered through their fingers. The beams illuminated a vast basement with a crusty old electric furnace at the center, stone cold. Along one wall stretched a long workbench, three feet deep, littered with rusty hand tools covered in cobwebs. Two additional sets of stairs, widely separated, led up to the main floor, apparently to opposite ends of the house.

"Well, that's weird enough," Kathy whispered.

"What?"

"Two sets of stairs heading up from a basement? Never seen that before."

"Look at the size of this place," Pete mumbled. "It's a *mansion*, remember?"

That made sense. Kind of.

Between the two flights of stairs were four closed doors. At some point, it appeared, the Wainrich family must have divided up the raw basement space.

Pete sidled over to the first door. "Whaddaya think's in here?"

Kathy followed, fighting her trepidation with every step. Her brother pushed open the door and stepped in, projecting light into a tiny bedroom. Inside was a bed covered with a chocolate-colored duvet, a small table and lamp, and a set of half-open dresser drawers that turned out to be full of clothes, all neatly folded. Plus closets, their doors splayed wide open, jam-packed with even more clothing on hangers.

"They left everything behind," Pete murmured.

"Uh-huh. Just like Roberta said." Kathy ran a finger across the top of the dresser to find dust a quarter inch thick. "*E-e-e-ew.*"

"What's behind door number two, I wonder?" Pete joked.

"Very funny, I'm sure."

Opening all the remaining doors one by one revealed a small bathroom with a shower stall—no tub—and two additional bedrooms. All very neat and all *very* dusty. They closed the door of the third bedroom and stood outside on the basement floor.

"Why would a rich family build three bedrooms in this yucky basement?" Kathy asked. "There must be enough *nice* bedrooms upstairs. The kind with windows—sunlight, fresh air, little things like that."

"They probably had lots of company," Pete said, his voice

low. "But imagine: the Wainrich family departed more than half a century ago, leaving the mansion and all this stuff to rot away. I'm surprised that—"

Somewhere in the manor, they heard the distinct sound of a door squeaking on its hinges. "What was *that?*" Kathy asked, almost gagging on her words.

"We've got company," Pete whispered. His jaw slackened.

They killed their phone flashlights, plunging themselves into total darkness.

"We're not alone, are we?" Kathy hissed. "We never were."

Worse, retreating through the glass hatch wasn't an option. To escape, they would have to access the manor's first floor, and even then . . .

"Weird, huh?"

"No fooling. How are we gonna get out of here?"

"Who's leaving?" Pete replied. Nothing much ever seemed to bother her brother, except confined spaces, which could make him panic, and being hugged, which he basically hated. "We're here to find out who—or what—is haunting this mansion. Now we're in. Follow me."

"Follow you? I can't even *see* you."

"Just stay close. I'm heading over to the stairs."

With only his feet and outstretched hands to guide him, Pete glided across the concrete floor, silent as the proverbial grave. Kathy hesitated, listening for him—*He's so quiet*—before setting off for the closer of the two sets of stairs. She began negotiating them one step at a time. Pete had to be somewhere in front, she figured. She counted sixteen steps up before her nose bumped into a— *Door?*

"Pete! Where *are* you?" she called out in an urgent whisper.

"Right here," he replied. From the far, far side of the basement.

"Tell me you're not serious. *You're at the wrong door—*"

"You're on the wrong set of stairs!"

At that second, a clock—it must have been huge, a tall grandfather clock maybe—chimed from somewhere within the mansion. The sound resonated, deep and jarring, down into the basement. *Bong . . . bong . . . bong . . . bong . . .*

Kathy's hand flew to her mouth.

Bong . . . bong . . . bong . . . bong . . .

Her mind raced. *How could a clock left unwound for six decades be chiming?* What the heck!

Bong . . . bong . . . bong . . . bong . . .

Midnight! Whispering no longer seemed viable. "We gotta get out of here!" she called out.

"Go through the door," Pete said in a rush. "Turn left. I'll be there."

She choked out the words. "Are we—are you *sure?*"

"Trust me! I'm heading onto the main floor. Now! You do the same."

Kathy grasped the doorknob and turned it ever so slowly. Then she pulled, cracking the door open a couple of inches. It creaked. She angled her head and peeked through the narrow opening. Too dark to see a thing. She opened it wider, and took one cautious step in . . .

Something moved.

I hope you have enjoyed this sneak peek at book 10 in
The Mystery Searchers Book Series

The Haunting of Wainrich Manor

BIOGRAPHY

Barry Forbes began his writing career in 1980, eventually scripting and producing hundreds of film and video corporate presentations, winning a handful of industry awards along the way. At the same time, he served as an editorial writer for Tribune Newspapers and wrote his first two books, both non-fiction.

In 1997, he founded and served as CEO for Sales Simplicity Software, a market leader which was sold two decades later.

What next? "I always loved mystery stories and one of my favorite places to visit was Prescott, Arizona. It's situated in rugged central Arizona with tremendous locales for mysteries." In 2017, Barry merged his interest in mystery and his skills in writing, adding in a large dollop of technology. The Mystery Searchers Family Book Series was born.

Barry's wife, Linda, passed in 2019 and the series is dedicated to her. "Linda proofed the initial drafts of each book and acted as my chief advisor." The couple had been married for 49 years and had two children. A number of their fifteen grandchildren provided feedback on each book.

Contact Barry: barry@mysterysearchers.com

ALSO BY BARRY FORBES

The Mystery Searchers Book Series

BOOK 1: THE MYSTERY ON APACHE CANYON DRIVE

A small child wanders out onto a busy Arizona highway! In a hair-raising rescue, sixteen-year old twins Tom and Suzanne Jackson save the little girl from almost certain death. Soon, the brother and sister team up with their best friends, Kathy and Pete Brunelli, on a perilous search for the child's family and her past. The intrigue deepens as one mystery splits into two, forcing the teenage sleuths to deploy surveillance technology along Apache Canyon Drive. The danger level ramps up with the action, and "the mystery searchers" are born.

BOOK 2: THE GHOST IN THE COUNTY COURTHOUSE

A mysterious "ghost" bypasses the security system of the Yavapai Courthouse Museum and makes off with four of the museum's most precious Native American relics. At the invitation of the museum's curator, the mystery searchers jump into the case and deploy a range of technological tools to discover the ghost's secrets. If the ghost strikes again, the museum's very survival is in doubt. A dangerous game of cat and mouse ensues.

BOOK 3: THE SECRETS OF THE MYSTERIOUS MANSION

Heidi Hoover, a good friend and the star newspaper reporter for the *Daily Pilot*, Prescott's local newspaper, introduces the mystery searchers to a mysterious mansion in the forest—at midnight! The mansion is under siege from unknown "hunters." Who are they? What are they searching for? Good old-fashioned detective work and a couple of hi-tech tools ultimately point toward the truth, but time is running out . . .

BOOK 4: THE HOUSE ON CEMETERY HILL

There's a dead man walking, and it's up to the mystery searchers to figure out why. That's the challenge laid down by Mrs. Leslie McPherson, a successful but eccentric Prescott businesswoman. The mystery searchers team up with their favorite local detective and use some hi-tech gadgets to spy on some equally high-tech criminals at Cemetery Hill. It's a perilous game—with very high stakes.

BOOK 5: THE TREASURE OF SKULL VALLEY

Suzanne discovers a map hidden in the pages of an old classic book at the thrift store where she works. It's titled "My Treasure Map" and leads past Skull Valley, twenty miles west of Prescott, and out into the high desert country—to an unexpected treasure. "Please help," a note on the map begs. The mystery searchers rely on the power and reach of the internet to trace the movement of people and events—from half a century earlier.

BOOK 6: THE VANISHING IN DECEPTION GAP

A text message to Kathy sets off a race into the unknown. "There are pirates operating out here, and they're dangerous. I can't prove it but I need your help." Who sent the message? Out where? Pirates! In a railway yard? The mystery searchers dive in, but it might be too late. The sender has vanished into thin air.

BOOK 7: THE GETAWAY LOST IN TIME

A stray dog saves the twins from a dangerous predator on the hiking trail at Watson Lake. In a surprising twist, the dog leads the mystery searchers to the suspicious recent death of Hilda Wyndham—and a crime lost to the passage of time. They join the Sheriff's Office of Yavapai County and Heidi Hoover, the star reporter of the *Daily Pilot*, in a search for unknown perpetrators past and present.

BOOK 8: THE HUNT FOR THE ELUSIVE MASTERMIND

The mystery searchers embark on one of their strangest cases—the kidnapping of the wife of one of Prescott's most prominent bankers. The mystery deepens as baffling questions emerge: Who are the kidnappers—beneath their disguises? What happened to the ransom money? And it soon becomes clear that the hostage may not be the only person in danger . . .

BOOK 9: THE LEGEND OF RATTLER MINE

In a rocky ravine north of the Flying W Dude Ranch, the mystery searchers save an unconscious man from certain death. Little do they know that they're about to step into a century-old legend that's far more dangerous than it first appears. Does Rattler Mine really exist? If it does, exactly where is it? And who is the mysterious man—or woman—willing to risk everything for it . . . no matter the cost?

BOOK 10: THE HAUNTING OF WAINRICH MANOR (COMING SPRING, 2022)

It's the Chief's birthday party, and the Jackson/Brunelli families gather to celebrate at his favorite restaurant in the Hassayampa Inn. Little do they know that they are about to cross paths with the charming Mrs. Roberta Robertson, who will introduce the mystery searchers to their most puzzling case yet. Someone is haunting an abandoned mansion—*but who and why?*

BOOK 11: THE DAYLIGHT HEIST ON WHISKEY ROW (COMING SUMMER, 2022)

Stay tuned!

DON'T FORGET...

Don't forget to check out
www.MysterySearchers.com

Register to receive updates on The Mystery Searchers Family Book Series. You'll also find a wealth of information on the website, including stills and video scenes of Prescott, reviews, press releases, rewards, and more.

Questions or comments? My email address: barry@mysterysearchers.com

Are you enjoying this series? Please do me a huge favor and do a quick review. They really make a difference!